Christmas Murders
Copyright © 2024 by S.F. Baumgartner

All rights reserved. No part of this publication may be reproduced or transmitted in any form or by any means, mechanical or electronic, including photocopying or recording, or by any information storage and retrieval system, or transmitted by email without permission in writing from the author.

NO AI TRAINING: Without in any way limiting S.F. Baumgartner [and Represent Publishing] exclusive rights under copyright, any use of this publication to "train" generative artificial intelligence (AI) technologies to generate text is expressly prohibited. The author reserves all rights to license uses of this work for generative AI training and development of machine learning language models.

Neither the author nor the publisher assumes any responsibility for errors, omissions, or contrary interpretations of the subject matter herein. Any perceived slight of any individual or organization is purely unintentional. Brand and product names are trademarks or registered trademarks of their respective owners.

ISBN 979-8-9911287-5-9
Library of Congress Control Number: 2024921371

FB PUBLISHING

Edited by Brilliant Cut Editing and Represent Publishing

Cover Design by 100bookcovers.com

CHRISTMAS MURDERS

CHRISTMAS MURDERS

A Mystery

S.F. BAUMGARTNER

FB PUBLISHING

AUTHOR'S NOTE

To all readers, especially residents and those familiar with the state of Florida, I wish to clarify that the town of Pine Grove is a purely fictional creation for this novella. (or series/book)

All characters and events depicted in this novel are born from my imagination. Any resemblance to actual people, living or dead, or to real-life events is entirely coincidental.

"Men make counterfeit money; in many more cases, money makes counterfeit men."

- Sydney J. Harris.

DECEMBER 21

CHAPTER 1

Detective Kylie Cassidy stood on the county courthouse's worn limestone steps and faced Aiden, who had a hand on her arm. "No, I've told you before. I can't help you."

The late afternoon sun cast long shadows across the wide plaza, glinting off the polished brass fixtures at the building's grand entrance. A gentle breeze rustled the old oak trees lining the sidewalk, carrying with it the faint sounds of traffic from the bustling downtown street beyond.

Aiden's fingers tightened around her arm, his eyes flashing. "Come on, KC."

"Let go of me." She tried to pull away without causing a scene.

A deep voice cut through the tension. "Is there a problem?"

KC pivoted. It took a moment to place him—the special agent she'd met at a crime scene months ago. *What was his name again?*

Aiden's grip held strong as he glared at the newcomer a few steps above them. "None of your business. Why don't you keep walking?"

The agent's eyes narrowed, recognition crossing his face. "Detective, is everything all right?"

KC took a deep breath and shook off Aiden's hand. "No problem here. Thanks for your concern, agent." She turned back to Aiden. "Go. We'll talk another time."

Splotches mottled Aiden's face. He lurched toward the agent, spitting out a string of curses. "This doesn't concern you, Fed."

"Aiden!" she snapped. "I said go. Now."

For a tense moment, Aiden loomed there like he might argue further. Then, with a final glare, he stomped off.

KC pasted on an apologetic smile. "I'm sorry about that. Aiden's...Well, he's a family friend. We went to the same school, grew up together. He can be a jerk sometimes."

He smiled. "No need to explain, Detective, uh, Casey, is it?"

"Cassidy. Agent?"

"Nathan Tanner. But you can call me Nate or Tanner."

"Okay, Tanner. My friends call me KC. That's probably why you thought my name was Casey. I hope you found the girl."

She'd responded to an auto accident early in the year only to find the driver killed execution style. Then Tanner and a younger agent showed up, working on an abduction case. She had gotten them a lead. In the end, the sheriff said to close the case when the perp was killed in a shoot-out. Details were murky.

Tanner squinted, then relaxed. "Oh, yes, she's doing well. Thanks for your help."

"Just doing my job. Are you, uh, here on a case?"

He stepped down two more of the courthouse stairs to stand level with her. "Yeah, testifying on a case. You? This is a bit far from your stomping ground, isn't it?"

"I dropped off some paperwork at the sheriff's office." She gestured toward the building down the street. Thinking of the transfer request sent her heart racing. If the transfer didn't go through, she'd be out of a job come New Year. "Then the ASA Sullivan wanted to discuss a case, so..." She shrugged.

"Well, I'd better be going before they send out a search party," he quipped and started back up the stairs. "Good to see you!"

She chuckled. "Same here. I should be going too. You never know. They might find a body in Pine Grove while I'm gone." *As if it would happen, it's more than likely a petty theft.*

An hour later, she drove toward the Pine Grove substation. The Christmas spirit enlivened the town. Retailers blasted Christmas music. A giant Christmas tree with hundreds of ornaments shimmered in the town square. In front of it, a Santa and elf picture station beckoned the kids.

She parked, went inside, and headed to her office and the stack of case files awaiting her. Shoplifting, vandalism, a domestic dispute—the everyday of small-town crime. She reached for the top file. Her gaze drifted to the window overlooking the parking lot. Her hand hovered in midair.

A dark SUV with tinted windows caught her attention. A Tahoe, if she wasn't mistaken. She'd never seen it before, which was unusual in a town where she knew most vehicles by sight. The car idled before pulling away, its movement almost too casual.

She frowned, a slight chill running down her spine. In Pine Grove, unfamiliar faces were rare, and anonymous vehicles even rarer. An out-of-town visitor, maybe? It was the holiday season, after all.

DECEMBER 22

CHAPTER 2

The next morning, KC's eyes snapped open at precisely 6:00 a.m., her body attuned to the rhythm of early mornings after years on the force. She swung her legs over the side of the bed, stretched, and padded to the window. The sun, just beginning to peek over the horizon, already painted the sky in soft pink and orange.

"Another day, another dollar." She slipped into her running shoes.

The crisp morning air nipped at her skin as she jogged through Pine Grove's quiet streets. Her mind wandered to the case files waiting on her desk, the interviews scheduled for the day, and the nagging feeling she was missing something important.

As she rounded the corner back onto her street,

a flash of red caught her eye. A beat-up Ford Taurus crawled along the curb, keeping pace with her. Cop instincts kicked in, and she slowed, pretending to adjust her shoelace while studying the vehicle.

Aiden's car.

"No, I don't believe this." She straightened up, set her jaw, and marched toward her rented house. Just before reaching her front door, she spun on her heel, ready to confront him.

"Aiden!"

The Taurus was already speeding away, leaving only a trail of exhaust in its wake.

KC shook her head and blew out a breath. *Coward.* She unlocked her front door.

The hot shower did little to wash away her unease. As she toweled off, she caught her reflection in the mirror. Dark hair, hazel eyes, and a face that seemed to carry the weight of generations of law enforcement.

Her aunt's voice echoed in her mind: "You just turned thirty, still single. When are you going to settle down?"

She could almost see her disapproving frown, hear the litany of eligible bachelors from the church. KC had always wanted a family of her own, but she hadn't met Mr. Right yet. And she had a legacy to uphold, a calling to answer. Her father had died in the line of duty. Since his death, her mom struggled and finally succumbed to her drug addiction.

"Sorry, Aunt Mae," KC said to her reflection. For a woman who had never had children, Aunt Mae did a wonderful job as her substitute parent.

Thirty minutes later, KC strode into the Pine Grove Sheriff's substation, a paper cup of coffee in one hand and a case file in the other.

Deputy Johnson nodded a greeting as she passed. "Morning, Detective Cassidy. Your suspect's waiting in Interrogation Room 2."

"Thanks, Johnson. Any movement on the Hendrick case?"

"Nothing yet. But forensics should have something for us by this afternoon."

KC nodded, shifting gears as she approached the interrogation room. She took a deep breath, set down her coffee, and pushed open the door.

Gray Thompson sat at the metal table, his fingers drumming an impatient rhythm on its surface. He was younger than KC had expected, barely out of his teens, with a mop of unruly brown hair, and his gaze flickered around the room.

"Mr. Thompson." She slid into the chair across from him. "I'm Detective Cassidy. Thank you for coming in to speak with us today."

Thompson's leg bounced under the table. "Like I had a choice."

KC opened the file in front of her, taking her time as she flipped through the pages. She could feel Thompson's anxiety ratcheting up.

"Can you tell me about your relationship with Evergreen Financial Services?"

Thompson swallowed hard. "They're just some company I took out a loan with. What's this all about?"

She leaned forward. "We have evidence that suggests you've been less than truthful on your loan applications. Multiple applications, in fact, all with inflated income statements and falsified employment records."

"That's... that's not true," Thompson stammered, but his eyes couldn't quite meet hers.

"No?" She raised an eyebrow. "Because we have copies of the applications right here, along with statements from the employers you claimed to work for. Employers who have never heard of Gray Thompson."

"Come on." He rolled his eyes. "Everybody does that. It's no big deal."

People might inflate their earnings a bit, but they seldom made up employment. "It is a big deal.

It's fraud. And it's illegal to lie on financial documents."

His face paled. "It is?"

"I'm afraid so."

He ran a hand through his hair, his composure crumbling. "I didn't know what to do. I just needed the money, you know? My mom's sick, and the medical bills..."

Everyone had a sob story! She softened her tone. "I understand you might have been in a difficult situation, Mr. Thompson. But what you did is still a crime. However, if you're willing to cooperate, to tell us what happened and who, if anyone, helped you with this scheme, we might be able to work out a deal."

His eyes widened. "A deal? You mean, like, I wouldn't go to jail?"

"I can't promise anything." She spoke with caution. "But if you work with us, plead to a lesser charge, the judge might be more lenient. It's your best option right now."

He went quiet, his internal struggle playing out across his face. Finally, he slumped in his chair.

"Okay," he murmured. "Okay, I'll tell you everything."

A half hour later, she emerged, a full confession in hand. She nodded to Johnson. "Book him."

As she settled back behind her desk, her phone buzzed. A text flashed on the screen.

AIDEN

Need to talk. It's important.

She stared at the message. Her earlier encounter with his car stiffened her spine. She should ignore it, delete the message, and focus on her current cases. But curiosity got the better of her.

With a frustrated groan, she typed out a reply.

KC

One chance. Tonight, 8PM, Riverside Park. 10 minutes.

She hit send. Just what trouble had Aiden gotten himself in?

DECEMBER 22

CHAPTER 3

KC drummed her fingers on the steering wheel as she navigated the quiet streets. The sun had dipped below the horizon, the sky surrendering to hues of purple and orange. She glanced at her dashboard clock—7:43 p.m.

"What's so important?" she muttered, recalling Aiden's cryptic text.

The police scanner crackled to life. "Possible underage drinking at Riverside Park. Any units in the vicinity, please respond."

The Pine Grove substation was always short on staff. She was the only detective stationed there, and since Pine Grove had few crimes more serious than a misdemeanor, she responded to calls most of the time.

Her eyebrows shot up. Underage drinking at the park? She shook her head, a wry smile curving her lips. "Just my luck." She reached for the radio. "Cassidy responding."

"Copy that, Detective," the dispatcher's voice came through.

Soon, KC turned into the park entrance and scanned the area. The parking lot was empty, save for a few cars. But something caught her attention —a flicker of movement in her peripheral vision.

She slowed down, pretending to look for a parking spot, all the while keeping an eye on the source of the movement. There, hidden under the sprawling branches of an old oak tree, idled a dark Chevy Tahoe, a faint plume of exhaust visible in the cooling evening air.

The same SUV she spotted yesterday?

Her pulse quickened. The back plate was smudged, and she couldn't see if there was one in front. She maneuvered her personal car into a spot and kept her focus on the vehicle. Its headlights were off, but she could make out one silhouette inside.

What are you up to? She reached for her phone and snapped a few quick photos.

Grateful she'd taken her own car instead of the sheriff's cruiser, she took a deep breath and stepped out. She sauntered as if she were another visitor to the park, continuously maintaining a visual of the Tahoe in her peripheral vision.

She walked toward the park entrance and glimpsed the figure in the SUV lifting something to his eyes. Binoculars? He must be watching something—or someone—in the park.

After she entered the park proper, she looked for Aiden. She also needed to check on the reported underage drinking and figure out what that guy in the SUV was up to. It was going to be a busy night.

KC stepped into the clearing at Riverside Park, her senses on high alert. The summer evening air carried the faint scent of cigarette smoke and something else she couldn't quite place. A trio of teens or college kids huddled on a park bench.

The moment they saw her, their eyes widened. Before she could even open her mouth, they bolted, darting toward the dense tree line bordering the park.

"Hey! Stop!" She broke into a run. Her feet pounded the soft earth as she pursued them into the woods. Branches whipped at her face and arms, but she pressed on, driven by instinct and years of training.

She was gaining on them, their heavy breathing and clumsy movements through the underbrush giving her an advantage. But as she was about to close the gap, she saw something out of the corner of her eye. She turned her head to catch whatever had distracted her.

In that split second, a figure materialized in front of her. She skidded to a stop. Her hand went to her holster before recognition dawned.

"Aiden?" she gasped, out of breath.

She glanced in the direction the kids had fled, then let out a huff, turning her full attention to her childhood friend.

"Okay, Aiden, talk."

Far from his usual composed self, he couldn't stay still, his body twitching with nervous energy. His gaze darted back and forth, never settling on one spot, as if he expected danger to leap out from every shadow.

"I'll be gone for a while," he blurted out.

She furrowed her brow. "What do you mean, 'gone'?"

He shook his head, still unable to meet her eyes. "Be careful. Can't trust anyone here."

"What are you talking about?" She crossed her arms. "Does this have to do with that speeding ticket you asked me to fix for you?"

"No, no." He dropped a card in her hand. "Call them."

"Them? What's going on? Are you in trouble?"

His restless movements ceased. His gaze focused on something behind her. His face drained of color.

She spun around, following his gaze, her hand once again moving to her weapon. "What is it? What are you looking at?"

She squinted into the darkness. Was that a shadow moving among the trees, or her imagination playing tricks on her?

When no answer came, she turned back to face him.

He was gone.

"Aiden!" she called out to his retreating figure sprinting toward the parking lot.

She gave chase. Her legs pumped hard as she tried to close the distance. But he was running as if his life depended on it. And he had a head start.

As they burst out of the tree line into the parking lot, the mysterious dark SUV sat ready. Its engine was already running, headlights cutting through the gathering dusk.

Aiden made a beeline for the vehicle, wrenched open the passenger door, and leaped inside.

"Aiden, wait!" She pushed herself to run faster.

Just before he slammed the door shut, he turned to her, fear clear in his face. He yelled something, but the SUV's engine drowned out most of his words. KC could only make out a fragmented warning: "Mo... mole... careful!"

The door slammed shut, and the SUV peeled out of the parking lot, tires screeching against the asphalt.

She skidded to a stop as the vehicle disappeared into the night, taking Aiden with it. She stood there, chest heaving, mind reeling. What did Aiden mean? Mole? Be careful? And who was the guy in that SUV?

DECEMBER 23

CHAPTER 4

KC stared at the case board in her small office, Aiden's fragmented warning from the night before still echoing in her mind. There was no plate, and the photos she took were too dim to make out the driver or run facial recognition. What to do?

"Detective!" Betsy, the dispatcher, stood by KC's door. "Ramirez just called in a DB out at the councilman's house."

Her hope for a short day just vanished. A DB —dead body. "Tell him I'm on my way. And to secure the scene. And alert the sheriff." She grabbed her badge and gun and rushed to her car while Betsy stepped out of her way with a "yes, ma'am."

When KC arrived at the house, Deputy Ramirez

was standing by his patrol car, face pale. Yellow crime scene tape fluttered in the breeze.

"Ramirez!" KC walked up. "What have we got?"

The young deputy swallowed hard. "It's... it's Councilman Prescott, Detective. Gunshot wound. I've never seen anything like it."

A councilman. This would be high-profile. Was this her life-line? She could solve this case. "Okay, thank you. I'll take it from here. Has the ME been called?"

"Yes, ma'am. They're on their way."

"Anybody else home?"

He gave a slight headshake. "I checked. Nobody was home except for the housekeeper who found the body. She's in the patrol car, pretty shaken up."

Prescott was widowed and lived alone. She didn't remember hearing any kids. "Live-in?"

"No, she comes every morning at seven." Ramirez consulted his notepad. "Name is Lucia Sanchez. But she had to take her son to the dentist, only time she could get, she said. Said the councilman okayed her to come in late."

"Did she touch anything?"

"No, she screamed and called 911."

"Thanks. I'll talk to her in a bit." She needed to

check out the body and scene first. The body was in the backyard, just outside of the lanai. "Ramirez, page all available units to come and canvass the area."

"Yes, ma'am."

As KC ducked under the tape, the crunch of gravel announced another arrival. She turned to see Detective Frank Morales from the main office climbing out of his car.

"Cassidy." The chubby man in his fifties waved. "You could use some help on this one."

She bristled. "I appreciate the offer, Detective Morales, but I can handle—"

"This isn't an offer." Morales cut her off. "Sheriff called me in. This is a high-profile, all-hands-on-deck case."

She bit back a retort. "Understood. I was just about to examine the body. Care to join me?"

"Let's!" Morales approached and kneeled beside it. "Gunshot wound to the chest," he murmured. "Close range, by the looks of it. This wasn't random. This was personal."

"Agreed." Her shadow fell over the victim's feet. "I know he was widowed. Any kids, do you know?"

Morales shook his head. "Hey, I moved here from Miami not that long ago."

"Right." She made a note on her phone to check for next of kin. "I don't know if he had any enemies."

"We'll need to chat with his colleagues and employees. In a town this size, everyone's a suspect until proven otherwise."

She surveyed the surroundings. Something glinted in the grass a few feet away. She went over, took a picture, then picked up the metal object—a small, ornate cuff link—with her gloved hand.

"What do you got?" Morales stepped closer to peer over her shoulder. "Well, well," he muttered. "Our councilman had expensive taste."

"Or maybe it belonged to our killer," she suggested. "Either way, it's our first solid lead."

KC bagged the evidence as the medical examiner's van pulled up. Dr. Bill O'Bannon, the bald and slim medical examiner, walked toward them.

"Morning, Detectives." He didn't smile. "What have we got?"

"The ME himself. This is big, Cassidy," Morales whispered, as if she didn't already know. Normally, the ME sent out death investigators to the scenes. Only high-profile cases warranted the appearance of the ME himself.

KC filled the doctor in on their initial observations as Dr. O'Bannon began his preliminary examination.

"Time of death, last night between six and midnight," the ME reported. "I'll know more once I get him back to the lab."

The doctor examined the body some more and didn't see anything else suspicious. So, KC went to interview the housekeeper. Sanchez didn't have anything to add. "No, nothing unusual." "No, didn't see nobody." "No, didn't see nothing." KC sighed. She made sure her contact information was current, then let her go.

Before Morales tried to take more control, she went to him. "Mind if I take point on interviewing the councilman's staff?"

He studied her before nodding. "All right, but I want to be kept in the loop. And, Cassidy? Watch yourself. Cases like this... they have a way of getting complicated fast."

"I'm doing a walk-through of his house." KC headed toward the house to learn more about the deceased. Morales followed her. The door opened to an entryway. To the right were two rooms with a guest bathroom in between. The guest rooms were empty. To the left was the laundry room with a door to the garage. She turned her head and saw another bedroom with an en suite bath. Also untouched. Inside the great room, with its dining table, living room, and open kitchen, all looked undisturbed. The sliding door to the lanai was closed. Finally, she went to the master. This huge room with a bath eclipsed her living room. She went back out.

"Keys and a glass of wine here." She pointed to the items on the kitchen counter.

"Here's a briefcase." Morales picked it up with his gloved hand from the floor next to the counter and opened it. He rummaged through it. "Nothing of note. But we should take it in."

KC surveyed the whole great room. "Nothing seems to be disturbed. No struggle. He came home, poured himself a glass of wine, then what? Something drew him out. A friend, somebody came by."

Since the body was found outside of the lanai, she returned there. "Ah, here's another wine glass. He was here, and someone showed up. A friend? He went to get another glass of wine for his guest. Something happened. An argument? Got heated. They got up. Maybe the guest was leaving, and he followed him and got shot?"

"Or the killer forced him out and shot him," Morales opined.

"Let's see what CSU comes up with." She didn't notice any photo of a family member other than one with his late wife in his room. Safe to say he had no kids. Still, she had to notify next of kin.

"Well, you take the staff, and I'll talk to his colleagues, okay?" Morales asked.

"On it."

Aiden warned her not to trust anyone, and now the councilman was murdered. Did this have anything to do with his warning?

DECEMBER 23

CHAPTER 5

Just before noon, KC sat at her desk, the crime scene photos spread out before her. Canvass didn't yield anything. The cuff link glinted in one of the images, taunting her with its secrets. Her phone rang, breaking her concentration.

"Detective Cassidy," she answered.

"Detective, it's Meg with the ME office. Dr. O'Bannon has preliminary findings on the Councilman Prescott—"

She didn't wait for the invitation. "On my way." She hung up.

Morales was lurking around the squad room.

"Hey, Morales," she called out. "O'Bannon has something. Want to check it out?"

"Sure." He got up and headed out the door.

She drove him to the morgue in her car.

Dr. O'Bannon greeted them as they entered. "Afternoon, Detectives. Thanks for coming so quickly."

"What do you have, Doc?" Morales asked.

The ME led them to the examination table where Prescott's body lay. "Cause of death is definitely the gunshot wound to the chest, as we suspected. But there's more." He pointed to some marks on Prescott's wrists. "See these abrasions? He was restrained before he was killed."

KC leaned in for a closer look. "This wasn't a heat-of-the-moment thing. It was premeditated."

"Looks that way." O'Bannon nodded. "And something else. I found traces of a substance on his clothes. Sent it to the lab for analysis, but my gut says it's cocaine."

Morales whistled low. "Prescott mixed up in drugs? That's a scandal waiting to explode."

"Thanks, Doc. This is helpful. Anything else?"

"Just one more thing." O'Bannon pointed to the bullet wound. "Based on the angle of the wound and powder residue, I'd say your shooter is left-handed. And probably around five ten to six feet tall."

She jotted this in her notebook. "Thank you. Keep us posted on the lab results."

"Merry Christmas, Detectives!"

They wished him the same and left the morgue. Morales strode alongside her. "So, what should we do next?"

"Dig deeper into Prescott's finances and connections." She got in the car and started it. "If he was involved with drugs, there has to be a money trail."

He slid into the passenger side. "True. Let's follow the money."

Back at the station, Morales handed KC a file. "I meant to give you this earlier. Info on that cuff link. It's part of a limited edition set. Only fifty were made. Sold exclusively at Hartley's Jewelers in the city."

"That's a start. Did you get a list of buyers?"

He shook his head. "Not yet. Owner's being cagey about confidentiality. Need a warrant."

She frowned. "We'll probably have to wait till after Christmas."

After he walked out, her thoughts drifted back to Aiden. She needed to find out more about what he said by "be gone for a while," but how? She'd have to retrace his steps from the night he vanished. Her first stop was his apartment. She sprang up and headed out.

Ten minutes later, she knocked on Aiden's door, more out of habit than expectation.

It creaked open slightly.

Heart racing, she drew her gun.

"Aiden?" she called out. "It's KC. Are you here?"

Silence greeted her.

She pushed the door open wider and entered. What a mess—drawers pulled out, papers strewn about, cabinets hanging open. Someone was looking for something.

While she surveyed the chaos, her phone rang. An unknown number.

"Detective Cassidy."

"Ky... it's... den." Heavy static garbled the familiar voice.

Her heart leaped. "Aiden? Is that you? Where are you?"

"Can't... Long." His voice was urgent, breaking up between bursts of static. "Listen... Ghost... Not... Eration... Pres... Involved... Care... Trus..."

The line went dead.

KC stared at her phone. What was Aiden trying to say? Something about a ghost? And Prescott being involved?

She considered calling Sheriff Hawkins, but

hesitated. Aiden's mole warning echoed in her mind. Could they have a mole in the department?

Keeping her discoveries to herself for now, KC headed back to the station. She'd have to piece together what she knew without raising suspicion.

Right after she walked into her office, her phone rang again.

"Cassidy," Sheriff Hawkins asked as soon as she answered. "Any progress on the Prescott case?"

"Some. The ME found traces of what might be cocaine on Prescott's clothes. And we've got a lead on the cuff link recovered from the scene."

"Cocaine?" He let out a low whistle. "Prescott was into drugs?"

"It's too early to say for sure," she hedged. "We're still waiting on the lab results."

"All right, keep me posted. And, Cassidy? I don't have to tell you how important this case is. Might want to cancel or rearrange your Christmas plans. The mayor wants this solved yesterday."

"Understood, sir." She ended the call. Holidays. That reminded her to call Aunt Mae about the festive meal.

The cuff link, Prescott's murder, the possible drug connection, Aiden's cryptic call. Was it possible they were all connected? If so, why? And more importantly, who could she trust?

DECEMBER 23

CHAPTER 6

The staff interviews yielded nothing. They all had solid alibis and none had anything to offer. The councilman had been jovial as always and appeared untroubled. No problem at work. No money problem anyone knew of.

A knock on the doorframe startled KC. Morales leaned against it, two cups of coffee in hand. He gestured one to her. "Thought you could use a pick-me-up."

He'd probably be around as long as the case was open. That alone would be an incentive to close it. "Thanks." She accepted the steaming cup. "I was thinking about the case."

He scanned the case board. "Any leads on where Prescott might have gotten the cocaine?"

"Not yet. We should start by looking into his known associates, see if anyone had ties to the drug trade."

"Good idea. I've got some contacts in Narcotics. I'll reach out, see if they've heard anything about new players in town."

The moment Morales turned to leave, she stilled. "Hey, Morales? You don't think this could have anything to do with the Ghost, do you?"

The Ghost, a notorious criminal mastermind, had topped the Most Wanted Lists. Hadn't Aiden said Ghost last night?

Morales froze and turned back, coffee cup extended like a shield. "The Ghost? That's a name I haven't heard in a while. Why would you think that?"

"Just a hunch." Her cup warmed her palm. "She's in federal custody, but her network was vast. Maybe some of her old associates are trying to fill the power vacuum."

"That's... an interesting theory." He sipped his coffee, somehow still managing to frown. "But the Ghost's case is way above our pay grade. Let's focus on what we know for now."

After he left, she slugged her drink before grabbing her jacket. She needed to talk to someone who might have a better pulse on the town's underbelly.

The Rusty Nail was quiet this early in the day, but her informant, Jimmy, nursed a beer at the far end of the bar. A dingy Christmas tree with a few symbolic ornaments leaned to one side in a corner. Jimmy still sported his shaggy hairdo, just like the day she arrested him for drug possession.

"Hey, Jimmy." She slid onto the stool next to him. "How's business?"

He snorted. "You're not here to check on my welfare, Detective. What do you want?"

She leaned in close. "What do you know about cocaine coming into town?"

His eyebrows shot up, and he sat back. "Nothing. I ain't touching that stuff."

"I'm not saying that. What do you know?"

Jimmy shrugged. "We don't see much of that around here."

"Come on, Jimmy. You hear things."

He sighed, glancing around before whispering. "There's been talk. New supplier, high-grade stuff. It's not street level. This is for the suits, you know?"

KC's brows furrowed. "Any names associated with this new supplier?"

"Nah." Her informant shook his head. "But

word is it might be linked to the Ghost's network. You know, that big-time criminal they caught a while back?"

Her face remained impassive. "Thanks, Jimmy. You've been helpful."

As she left the bar, her phone buzzed with a text.

> **UNKNOWN NUMBER**
>
> What you seek is closer than you think. Watch your step, Detective.

Whoever had texted her blocked the number. Chances were that it was a burner. She scowled at the phone before getting in her car to drive back to the station.

Morales was waiting for her.

Oh, brother! That's what I get for ignoring his calls.

"Where have you been?" he demanded. "I've been trying to reach you."

"Sorry. I was following up on a lead." She went to her desk. "What's up?"

Morales narrowed his eyes. "We got the full tox screen back on Prescott."

"How's that possible? It's Christmas holiday,

the day before Christmas Eve. And even when it's a regular day, it takes days."

"Well, it's the councilman. I told the sheriff. He called the mayor, who then called the governor, and I don't know who else he called to light a fire. Anyway, it's back. It wasn't just cocaine. They found traces of a new designer drug in his system. The lab's never seen anything like it."

A new drug, a possible connection to the Ghost's network... It all started to fit.

"Also," he continued, "I did some digging into Prescott's finances. There are some irregularities, large deposits from unnamed sources."

"Sounds like we need to take a closer look at his accounts." Morales nodded. "I'll get a warrant."

After he left, she jotted down what they knew so far. She couldn't ignore the connection to the Ghost. Aiden mentioned it, and so did Jimmy. Potential corrupt officials. Was this over her head?

And why did Aiden tell her not to trust anyone? That reminded her of the card. She dug it out and called the number. FBI Task Force 629.

DECEMBER 23

CHAPTER 7

Against her better judgment, KC had left a message for someone from the task force to return her call. A federal task force should always have someone answering the phone. So, perhaps it was a fake, or maybe they were off.

Most nonessential personnel left the station. Most places were closed. She'd take a chance and stop by the sleek offices of Harding Development, a local real estate company. According to Prescott's records, he had several meetings with Marcus Harding, the company's CEO, in the weeks leading up to his death.

KC flashed her badge at the receptionist, who was packing up to leave. "Detective Cassidy to see Mr. Harding. He's expecting me."

She was prepared to hear that Mr. Harding was on holiday. But she was in luck. Minutes later, she was ushered into a plush corner office bathed in the warm glow of the setting sun with a view of the town square.

Harding, a man in his fifties with salt-and-pepper hair and a crisp suit, stood from behind his desk. Tension in his shoulders betrayed his annoyance at the late interruption. "Detective." He offered his hand, his smile not quite reaching his eyes. "To what do I owe this unexpected pleasure?"

KC matched his smile. "I'm following up on a few things regarding Councilman Prescott. I understand you two met frequently?"

Harding's smile almost faltered. "Ah, yes. Terrible business, that. Bart and I had a few meetings about potential developments in the county. Nothing out of the ordinary."

"I see." But he used Prescott's first name. "And these meetings, they were all about business?"

His eyes narrowed. "Of course. What else would they be about?"

She shrugged. "It's just that we found some interesting deposits in the councilman's accounts. Large sums, from unnamed sources. I don't suppose you'd know anything about that?"

Harding's left eye twitched, and he tugged at his

collar. "I... I'm not privy to Bart's personal finances, Detective. Our dealings were strictly professional."

"Of course." KC watched him closely. "One last thing, Mr. Harding. Does the name 'Ghost' mean anything to you?"

The color drained from his face. "I think this interview is over. If you have any more questions, you can direct them to my lawyer."

She walked out of the office, mentally replaying the interview. Harding's reaction to the Ghost's name was telling. Normal people wouldn't know the name referred to a notorious criminal. Harding knew something. Was this proof enough that the Ghost was involved?

Back in her car, her phone buzzed with a text.

MORALES

Got something big.

So much for having an early day. KC headed back to the station. One week. She only had one week to solve the case. The mayor's nephew, a newly promoted detective, would replace her in the new year. No, they hadn't said it outright, but only one detective worked in the station since the beginning of time.

"Here you are!" Morales stood up from *her* desk.

She clenched her jaw. What was he doing there?

"Oh, I was just sitting here. Sorry. Remember those rejected city development projects we were looking into?" He went around to flop down on a visitor's chair.

KC sat in her chair. "Go on."

"Well, I did some digging. Turns out, each of those rejected projects had a competing proposal that got approved instead. Guess who submitted those proposals?"

"Who?"

"Shell companies," he said. "All traced back to one holding company—Grove Enterprises."

She locked her hands in her lap. "And let me guess, Grove Enterprises has some interesting connections?"

"Bingo. The CEO is none other than our dear Councilman Roberts's brother-in-law."

"Oh, geez." The chair rocked her. "So Roberts rejects competing projects, and his family benefits?"

"It gets better," he continued. "Mayor Nell Hutchins? Her husband is on the board of Grove Enterprises."

Her pulse quickened. "They're both in on it. But how does this connect to Prescott's death?"

"That's where it gets murky." Morales leaned back, running a hand through his hair. "The last project Prescott was working on before he died? It would have directly competed with Grove Enterprises's biggest development yet."

"Let me guess, Prescott was pushing for it hard?"

"He was the only one on the council fighting for it. Said it would 'bring real change to Pine Grove.'"

KC stilled her chair. "So we've got motive. But it still feels like we're missing something."

"Yeah," he agreed. "We need to talk to Roberts and Hutchins. See if we can rattle them with this info."

She stood up. "Let's go! If we're lucky, we might catch them at Palmetto Diner. That is, if they haven't left town for the holidays."

This provided a good lead as far as motive for murdering Prescott. However, it still didn't explain the deposits in his accounts or the drug residual on his clothing.

DECEMBER 23

CHAPTER 8

KC stepped out of the station with Morales. The warm air carried the scent of nearby orange groves. Across Main Street, the town's Christmas tree stood fully lit, its twinkling lights casting a festive glow over the square. The cheerful sight felt at odds with their grim task.

In the bustling Palmetto Diner, ceiling fans spun lazily overhead, and patrons sought refuge from the persistent Florida heat. KC surveyed the room, taking in the polished wooden booths, framed photos of local dignitaries, and the low murmur of hushed conversations among the more subtle details.

Doris, the waitress/manager, appeared as soon

as KC slid into the booth across from Morales. "The usual, Detective?"

"Yes, please."

"You bet. And you, sir?"

Morales scanned the menu board. "I'll have a BLT, please."

Doris took the orders and walked away. Thanks to the five-star reviews on multiple eatery sites, the diner was busy year round. Tourists, locals, and businessmen all liked to sample the local fare.

KC craned around. "I don't see the mayor or the councilman here."

"Then let's eat and head to the city hall where we'll find them."

Doris returned with her iced tea and Cobb salad and his BLT.

Morales took a bite of his sandwich and spoke around the mouthful. "Did you get a chance to look at Roberts's finances?"

"Not much on the surface. Pillar of the community, organizing the Christmas food drive, all that jazz. But..." She lowered her voice. "I only did a cursory search just before we left. I already saw some discrepancies."

"What kind of discrepancies?"

Iced tea washed down a bite of dry egg. "Large deposits that don't match up with his declared income. And get this—they coincide with the dates of several rejected city development projects."

His brows rose. "You think he's taking bribes to block projects?"

KC shrugged. "It's a theory. But we need more evidence before we can make any accusations."

"Okay, so we talk to him. Probably Mayor Hutchins too, since she'd have to be involved in those project decisions."

"Already set up interviews for this afternoon." She loaded avocado and chicken on her fork. "You take Roberts. I'll handle Hutchins?"

"Sounds good."

At City Hall, KC made her way to Mayor Hutchins's office. Volunteers were gearing up for the Christmas Eve festivities.

The mayor greeted her with a politician's smile. "Detective Cassidy, what brings you by on this beautiful day?"

KC took a seat across from her desk. Her gaze landed on Hutchins's tight grip of her pen. "I'm following up on a few things related to the councilman's case, ma'am. I was hoping you could clarify some information about recent city development projects."

"Of course." Hutchins launched into an explanation.

KC only half listened, more intent on the mayor's body language. "And the final decision always comes down to a vote between you and Councilman Roberts?"

"That's correct. Though we try to reach a consensus."

KC leaned forward. "I noticed several high-profile projects were rejected in the past year. The new community center, the orange grove preservation initiative... Can you tell me more about why those didn't pass?"

Something flashed across Hutchins's face before she composed herself. Was it anger? Or fear? "Each project is evaluated on its own merits. Sometimes they don't meet our criteria for approval."

"I see. These decisions, they wouldn't have anything to do with certain... financial incentives?"

"Of course not!" The mayor's tone cooled ten degrees. "I... I don't know what you're implying. Our decision-making process is transparent."

Time to venture onto thin ice. "Then you wouldn't mind providing documentation to support such claims?"

Hutchins stood. "This interview is over, Detective Cassidy. I would advise you to tread carefully. If you have any further questions, direct them to the city attorney."

A little later, KC walked into the substation. Morales sat in her office, his lips tight and shoulders hunched.

"How'd it go with Roberts?" She rounded her desk.

"Stone wall. He stuck to the party line about project evaluations and budget constraints. You?"

"Hutchins practically ran me out of her office when I mentioned financial incentives." She sat in her chair. "She's definitely hiding something."

"Yeah, well, so is half the town, it seems. I've been making calls all afternoon. Nobody wants to talk about those rejected projects or anything to do with the councilman."

"There has to be a connection here. The timing is too perfect."

"Maybe," he conceded. "But we need to be careful. We're dealing with powerful people."

"Exactly what the mayor warned me, but—"

Her phone cut her off.

She glanced at the screen and frowned. "I need to take this."

Morales stepped out to give her privacy.

She swiped to answer. "Yes, Pete."

"Hey, KC, uh, Detective." Pete Simmons, a deputy barely out of the academy, spoke in hushed staccato. "I... I think I saw something I shouldn't have. About the councilman."

Her pulse quickened. "What did you see?"

"I can't... I don't think... not over the phone."

They had gone to the same school. He had the body of a football player and played on the high school team. What had gotten him so scared? "It's okay. You can tell me."

Heavy breathing chuffed on the other end. "Can we meet? Football field, in an hour?"

"I'll be there," she promised.

DECEMBER 23

CHAPTER 9

KC twisted her grip on the steering wheel as she drove. Pete's cryptic phone call had put her on edge. What could he have seen about the councilman that had him so spooked?

She pulled into the empty parking lot. Floodlights cast long shadows across the high school football field. Pete's bulky silhouette stood out near the bleachers, his nervous pacing visible even from a distance.

"Pete," she called out.

He whirled around, eyes wide. "KC, I mean, Detective."

"KC is fine. We're not in the office. So, what's going on? What did you see?"

He glanced around, as if expecting someone to jump out of the shadows. "I was doing a late-night patrol—you know, routine stuff. I saw Councilman Prescott's car parked outside Whiskey Hollow."

She frowned. That seedy bar on the outskirts of town sure wasn't the kind of place you'd expect to find a councilman, especially a mayor pro tem. "Okay, and?"

"I thought it was weird, so I stuck around," he whispered. "About an hour later, Prescott came out, but he wasn't alone. He was arguing with this guy I've never seen before."

"Did you hear what they were saying?"

He palmed the back of his neck. "No, but... the other guy, he said something that made Prescott go pale. Then he handed Prescott an envelope. I couldn't see what was inside, but whatever it was freaked him."

Could this mysterious meeting be related to Prescott's murder? "Pete, this is important. Can you describe the man Prescott was with?"

"That's the thing. I couldn't see his face. He was wearing a hat, kept to the shadows. But the way he moved, how he held himself... it was like he wasn't even there, you know? Like a ghost."

"A ghost?" But this couldn't be the Ghost. She

was in federal custody. Was it someone in her pocket? This was a good lead. The man couldn't have been the one in the mysterious car that took Aiden away, could he? Anyhow, she needed to find out what was in the envelope and how and if it was connected to Prescott's murder.

"Yeah, but that's not why I didn't want to talk in the office. I didn't see the guy's face, but I saw his shadow get in a car. Not just any car, a squad car."

So Aiden was right. They had a mole, but who? "Thanks for letting me know. If you see this guy again or if you hear anything else, call me directly."

He nodded.

When KC got back to the station, Morales was still sitting at a borrowed desk. The word *mole* kept ringing in her ear. Could she trust Morales? Only as far as she could throw him, but she'd gauge his reactions. "Morales, we need to talk."

"What's up?"

She led him to her office. "We gotta consider the possibility the Ghost's network might be at work here."

He sucked in a short breath. His jaw muscle twitched. Was that fear? "Why? What did you hear?"

"Rumors. The Ghost's network could be connected to the local drug trade."

"The Ghost..." Morales rubbed his pudgy jaw. The rasp of day-old stubble grated. The twitch kept going. "That's not a name you hear thrown around lightly. It's more of a whisper, a boogeyman story that floats around the criminal underworld. And she is in federal custody now. So, there's no reason to worry about her connection."

"I heard she had lots of people in her pocket. What if she's still calling the shots?"

"I suppose. But it's all rumors and hearsay. Nothing concrete."

"What if her network is connected to Prescott's murder?"

"It's possible but be careful with this Ghost stuff. People who ask too many questions about it... Well, they tend to disappear."

A chill shivered down her spine. She stiffened as a fire ignited in her gut. This was her way of securing her future here, anyway.

"We need to dig deeper into this," she insisted. "If the Ghost is real and connected to Prescott, this could blow the whole case wide open."

"I still think we should focus on more concrete leads."

"Sure, we run down every lead. But also talk to some of the local dealers we've picked up recently."

Morales muttered a "yeah," stood up, and walked out as her phone buzzed.

Nathan Tanner.

She picked up her phone. "Cassidy."

"KC, Detective, Nate Tanner returning your call." His voice came through the line.

Her call? She searched her memory. "Uh, I didn't call you."

"You left a message on the task force line. I noticed it was you, so I took the liberty to return your call."

"Oh." Now this was interesting. "I was calling about Aiden Chambers. He gave me this card. Said he'd be away for a while and to call you guys."

Key-tapping sounds filled his pause. Then he got back on. "As far as I know, he's safe. Are you the case detective for the Bart Prescott murder?"

"Yes, and how'd you know about his death?"

"It's on the news."

Made sense. She might as well ask him about the Ghost. "Hey, there might be connections to a larger criminal network. I heard the Ghost was in federal custody. You guys know anything about it?"

The pause was longer this time. "Yeah, she is in our custody. Why do you ask?"

"It came up in our investigation."

"What makes you think the Ghost is involved?"

"Two witnesses mentioned something to that effect."

Another long pause. "If you'd like, I'll review what you have and get back to you."

Would she be going over her superiors again? If she was going to lose her job in the new year anyway, what difference did it make? "Will do. Thanks." She confirmed his email address, gathered all the documents, and sent them to Tanner.

"Hey, you wanna interview the drug dealers?" Morales called from the squad room. "They're ready."

She headed to the interrogation room. That occupied her next hour, but information about the Ghost remained elusive. Most of the suspects clammed up at the mention of the name. Others spoke of the Ghost with a mix of fear and awe. In the end, she didn't learn anything new.

As the sun began to set, she glanced out the window. Holiday lights twinkled along Main Street.

Her phone buzzed again. A text.

PRIVATE NUMBER

> We're watching you. Stop digging or join Prescott.

KC stared at her phone, the menacing text message still glowing on the screen. *Who are you?* She wanted to call the tech department. But she couldn't trust anyone in the department. Maybe, just maybe, Tanner could get the bureau to check?

DECEMBER 23

CHAPTER 10

"I don't want to ask... our tech—" KC stammered.

"Say no more. I'll ask Deanna, our tech, to trace it."

"Thank you!"

"But you've definitely rattled some cages. You must be on the right track, or they wouldn't be threatening you. Just be careful."

"I know." She thanked him and hung up. Staring at the screen wouldn't solve the case. Time to go down the financial rabbit hole before she went home. There had to be some records of something. She couldn't get the list of buyers of the cuff link until after the holiday. Following the money trail ought to give her something.

Hours later, KC rubbed her tired eyes and glanced at the clock on the wall. Already past eight?

"Come on. There's got to be something here." She flipped through another set of electronic documents. Just as she was about to call it a night, a line item caught her eye. She leaned in closer, her finger tracing the numbers.

"Wait a minute..."

She grabbed her phone, dialed Morales, and hung up right away. Could she trust him with this information? Should she follow it by herself? Her phone rang while she was pondering. *Dang it.* Morales must have seen her ID.

"Hey, did you call?" he asked as soon as she answered.

KC couldn't think of a good reason not to answer. Over the phone, the noise came through in faint, disjointed bursts—the low rumble of heavy objects dragging across the floor, the occasional clatter of something metallic hitting the concrete. Now and then, as a muffled echo, as if footsteps or voices were bouncing off an empty, cavernous space. It was distant, but chaotic, like a flurry of movement in a hollow, forgotten warehouse.

"Oh, I must have accidentally dialed you. Sorry." A lame excuse, if ever there was one.

"No, no, that's okay. You're still at the station? Did you find something in Prescott's finances?"

There was some commotion. The slamming of a door. Then the noise level went down.

"I did. Nothing important, anyway."

"Are you sure? You need me to come in?"

"Oh no. I'm packing up to go. Enjoy the rest of your evening." She wasn't going to tell him about what she found, but who could she tell?

"All right, then. Go home!" He hung up.

Her phone rang again. And Tanner's contact info lit the screen. She swiped to answer. "Did you find out who sent the text?"

"Not yet. Deanna's monitoring your phone. Next time it happens, she'll try to trace it. Uh, I'm calling about something else."

"Okay?" She was half reading what was on the screen.

"How would you like to work on a classified project?"

Her eyes stretched wide. "What? A classified project? I'm in the middle of a murder case."

"After reviewing what you have so far, we believe your case is connected to something bigger. So, we'd like you to work with us on this. If you agree, I'll meet you somewhere and brief you."

"You're not joking?" She stopped scrolling.

"Not at all."

Working with the FBI on a classified project? "Sure, I'm in. Do I need to go to Orlando?"

"No, I can go to you. Text me an address of somewhere private. Not your station."

She agreed and texted him her address. She wouldn't consider anywhere except her own house, private. Aunt Mae lived just down the street. She would borrow Sir Nick, her aunt's Doberman, for the evening.

Tanner did say the case was connected to whatever this classified case was. So, she saved all her research on a flash drive, packed up, and headed home.

When she came home from walking Sir Nick, he started barking before she even took the leash off him.

And the doorbell rang.

KC had Sir Nick by her side when she opened the front door. Tanner stood there on alert.

"Quiet, Sir Nick! He's a friend." She opened the screen door to let him in. "I hope you're not allergic to dogs."

"I'm good with animals." He stepped in and extended his hand, palm down, to let Sir Nick sniff.

So, he does know dogs.

After the ritual, Sir Nick determined Tanner was harmless. The dog left him alone.

KC invited Tanner to sit at the table where she had her laptop out. "If you haven't eaten yet, we can order something."

"No, that's fine, thanks. Let me explain the joint op with the DEA."

And he did over some snacks and coffee. Then it was KC's turn. "We've got a series of deposits made to an offshore account in the Cayman Islands. The amounts match with the funds supposedly rejected for that highway expansion project."

"So, you think your councilman was laundering money?"

She nodded and dipped a corn chip in salsa. "And not just small amounts. We're talking millions."

Tanner whistled.

Sir Nick cocked his head, perhaps thinking Tanner was calling him.

She motioned the gentle giant down on his mat by the sliding glass door. "And that's not all I've found. I've been cross-referencing these transactions with other local projects, and there's a pattern. Every major infrastructure project in the last five years has a corresponding set of offshore transactions."

"That's very good. I'll share what you have with the joint op team." A dollop of salsa dribbled from his nacho chip as his hands became animated. "We're looking at a systemic issue. Multiple officials, contractors."

"Yeah. I never thought something like this would happen in Pine Grove."

He scoffed. "Greed is a powerful motivator."

KC opened a new desktop with a new set of data documents. "Here's one more thing. I think the town's holiday charity drive is connected to all of this."

Tanner leaned forward. "The charity drive? How?"

"Look at the donation records." She pointed them out, leaving a greasy smear on her screen when she accidentally touched it. "The largest donations are coming from shell companies. The same ones are receiving the laundered money from the infrastructure projects."

"They're using the charity as a way to legitimize the dirty money. Clever."

"But why involve the charity at all?" She frowned. "Why not just keep the money offshore?"

He wiped his hands on a paper napkin, then squeezed it in a fist. "Because they're not just stealing. They're building a power base. The charity gives them influence, goodwill in the community. It's the perfect cover."

Oh! He's good. Who'd have thought of it that way?

He continued balling up the napkin. "These fit with the patterns we've seen in other small towns across the state. A network of corruption using local charities and infrastructure projects to launder money and build political influence."

"Other towns?" KC echoed. "You mean this isn't isolated to us?"

"I'm afraid not." He tossed the napkin wad to his other hand —the guy needed a fidget toy. "Uh, other teams are working on ops in other towns. The Bureau believes a larger organization's at play. One systematically targeting small towns like yours."

"Wow, so this is big, much bigger than just a murder case." "You can say that again."

Sir Nick let out a soft huff, stretched his front legs forward with a deep groan, then circled a few times before settling down near her, his eyes flicking toward KC's plate every so often.

KC reached down to give him a reassuring pat on the head. "Why didn't you want to meet in the station?"

"Because we think there's a mole. And we don't know how widespread this is."

"So, what do you want me to do?"

"Just do your job. We'll provide support."

"What about flushing out the mole?"

"We're working on that. Be careful and don't discuss this with anyone in the station." He stood to leave, giving Sir Nick a wave. "Watch your back. And Merry Christmas, if I don't see you again."

DECEMBER 24

CHAPTER 11

Still reeling from her conversation with Tanner, KC walked into the Pine Grove station the next morning. The corruption she'd uncovered stretched far beyond their small town. What daunting implications.

The Christmas tree in the station lobby didn't leave her spirits merry and bright. Her chances of having a half day off were dwindling by the minute. As she settled at her desk, her gaze fell on Morales outside in the squad room.

"Cassidy, got a minute?" Sheriff Hawkins stopped in her doorway, his presence unexpected but not unusual.

"Of course, Sheriff." She started to stand up.

He gestured for her to stay seated and sat across

from her. "How's the councilman case coming along?"

KC folded her arms, not rushing into responding. "We're making progress, sir. Following up on some leads related to the rejected project funding."

Hawkins flicked something off his equipment belt. "I've been hearing some concerns from the mayor's office. Seems like your investigation is ruffling feathers in high places."

A chill ran down her spine. "Sir, I'm just following the evidence—"

"I know, I know." He held up a hand. "But sometimes, Cassidy, the deeper you dig, the messier things get. Maybe it's time to take a step back, let things settle."

She let things settle long enough to draw a deep breath. "With all due respect, sir, I think we're close to a breakthrough. Backing off now could jeopardize the entire case."

The sheriff's eyes narrowed. "Just be careful. This town has a long memory, and you don't want to make enemies in high places."

Another warning. *Message received.*

After he left, KC followed up with tech about a possible door cam catching something in Prescott's neighborhood. They didn't have any good leads.

Either the image was too grainy or the driver or plate wasn't visible.

Cuff link. That had to wait until they had a warrant. She went over the timeline of the victim's last days. As best she could reconstruct, Prescott was last seen in the office. He went home. Somebody showed up, or something made him go out to the backyard. He was restrained, then shot.

Means. The perp policed his brass. CSU didn't find any casings. Autopsy recovered small fragments. She'd need to follow up with the lab to confirm the caliber.

Without a suspect, she couldn't tackle the opportunity, except that she believed it was someone Prescott had known. He wouldn't have gone out to meet the person if not.

Down to motive. Right now, she was going with this whole corruption-and-money-laundering scheme. If Prescott was laundering money, why was he killed? Money issues? Or, if he was a good guy, where did the money in his account come from?

Her phone buzzed her thoughts. Another text from an unknown number. Heart pounding, she opened the message.

UNKNOWN NUMBER

Stop digging, or you'll be buried with what you find.

She messaged Tanner about the text, hoping his tech could trace it.

"I've got some new leads on the councilman case." Morales walked into her office.

"What leads?"

He spread the papers on her desk. "I've been digging into Prescott's personal life. Turns out, he had some gambling debts. And get this—he was seen arguing with a known bookie days before his death."

Whoa. Her brows furrowed. She hadn't seen any gambling debts when she looked into Prescott's personal finances. And she was thorough. "This is the first I'm hearing about gambling debts. Where did this information come from?"

"CI. It's solid. We should focus on this angle."

Morales outlined his theory while doubt niggled her. The gambling angle seemed too convenient, too neat. Was he intentionally steering her away from the corruption trail she'd been following?

DECEMBER 24

CHAPTER 12

KC reviewed Prescott's financials again just to be sure she hadn't missed anything. Nothing in the financials or interviews with staff and friends suggested any gambling habits. Then she set in to review the physical evidence with fresh eyes.

"Merry Christmas, KC, Detective." Pete walked into the station. "I thought I drew the short straw. Shouldn't you be hanging out with your aunt by now?"

"Only if I can close the councilman case." She sidled up and whispered, "Any more news?"

He shook his head.

She continued down to the evidence locker, her steps echoing in the quiet hallway. After logging in on the terminal, she approached the locker, unlocked, and opened it. Her heart dropped to her stomach. The shelf where she meticulously placed the evidence bags from the Prescott case was empty.

"No, no, no." Grinding her teeth, she searched the other shelves. But it was futile. The bags containing the councilman's personal effects, the trace evidence they'd collected from the scene—they were all gone.

Reeling, she gripped the empty locker shelf. Who could have accessed it? And why? She pulled out her phone, hesitating before dialing Morales. She had to do this by the book.

"Morales," came the curt answer.

"KC here. We've got a problem. The evidence from the councilman case is missing."

"Missing? What do you mean, 'missing'?"

"You know—gone, disappeared, missing, not here."

There was a pause. "All right, sit tight. I'm heading down there. Don't touch anything and don't tell anyone else yet. We need to handle this carefully."

This was bad. The mole. It had to be the mole. But who could it be? She leaned against the wall, closed her eyes to concentrate. Who had access to the locker? The evidence clerk, the deputies, herself, Morales, and the sheriff. So, one of them did something to the evidence.

She'd rule out the sheriff. For now. He wasn't here often.

She opened her eyes. Something caught her attention—a paper scrap near the evidence locker. She gloved up and picked it up.

Neat block letters warned: "BACK OFF OR ELSE."

On hearing Morales's footsteps, she sealed it in an evidence bag—one of the few things she always had with her—and pocketed it. Trust no one—this was her new motto.

"So, what's missing?"

KC pointed to the empty locker. "Everything. Prescott's personal effects, the trace evidence we collected from the scene —it's all gone."

He cursed under his breath. "This is a major breach. Let's go ask the evidence clerk. Check the log to see if anyone signed out anything."

"Let's." She followed him, but there wouldn't be any records of it.

Pat, the fiftyish clerk with love handles, was tapping on the keyboard when they approached. "Hey, Detectives." He glanced up at them. "Help you?"

Morales folded his arms. "We need to see the evidence log."

Pat looked from KC to Morales. "You mean the paper backup?"

KC sighed. "Yes. Have you seen anyone coming back here in the last twenty-four hours?"

He tipped his head to one side. "Johnson logged something in. A necklace or something. Look online. There's a case number. That's all. I don't know about the overnight shift." He pulled out the logbook. "Here's the backup log."

She thanked him. They studied it.

Just as she had thought, there was no record of anyone signing it out. Thank goodness for electronic logs. The original items might be gone, but she had photos online.

"Let's go back to Prescott's house," Morales suggested. "Maybe we missed something there. We'll need to find some new evidence."

Unlikely, they'd find any new evidence, but it was something. Someone—the mole—stole the evidence. However, they needed to move forward.

Outside, twinkling lights and festive garlands adorned shop windows, holiday music played from near the town Christmas tree and photo booth, and the scent of peppermint and gingerbread wafted from the local café. Each scent, sight, and sound enlivened their town with the spirit of Christmas.

"I'll drive." She tapped her key fob to unlock her car, expecting him to go to the passenger side.

Instead, Morales kept walking. "I'll take mine. May be leaving from there. Meet you at the house in twenty."

Whatever. KC slid into her sedan and pushed the start button. At the first stop sign, she hit the brakes, but the car wasn't slowing down. She slammed on the brakes again. Again, with no effect. A horn blared from a vehicle she barely missed hitting. Heart pounding, she maneuvered the sedan to a tree. Fortunately, she wasn't going fast enough to cause a big impact. It stopped the car, though.

After her heart settled, she fought the airbag to get out.

"You okay?" Morales jogged over from his car stopped nearby.

"Yeah. No. I don't know." She braced her hands on the hood. "I think someone tampered with my car."

His face darkened. "This isn't a coincidence. Someone's trying to shut us down."

"But who?"

"I don't know." He shrugged.

"If they would try to kill me, I must be getting close."

"You sound determined."

"I am. Now, more than ever." She grabbed her things from the car. "Can you give me a ride back to the station? I need to take care of this mess."

"Sure." He walked her to his car. "But you know the clock is ticking. The brass wants this solved yesterday."

"Tell me about it."

Back at the station, she took care of her vehicle business, then ensured she was alone before calling Tanner.

"Are you okay?" he asked after hearing her updates.

"Yes, thanks."

"But you must know you're on the right track. Otherwise, they wouldn't be trying to silence you. You just need to be careful—trust no one."

"Did you find out who made those calls?"

"It was from a burner. Deanna is still monitoring your phone."

"Thanks. Oh, there was a note by the evidence locker. I don't want to send it to the lab to test for prints, since I don't know who to trust."

"Where's your car? Did you have a crime scene tech check the site and the car?"

"I had it towed to a garage. I haven't filed any report yet."

"I'll have it towed to our facility. Our tech will check it. And I'll come by tonight to pick up the note. We'll test it here. Unless you have plans for Christmas Eve."

"I do, but I'm not sure if it's happening now. See you later."

A heavy weight lifted off her shoulder. She opened her mouth to speak, but the Tahoe driving by caught her attention. She thanked Tanner again, hung up, shoved her chair back from her desk, and hurried outside. Did it mean Aiden was back?

DECEMBER 24

CHAPTER 13

KC sighed when a family got out of the Tahoe across the street. It was just a coincidence. After a couple of hours studying the online evidence log, she was confident they were complete, even though the physical evidence was missing. She made a backup copy.

Her phone buzzed, startling her out of her thoughts. She opened a text.

> DISPATCH
>
> Body found in Oakwood Park.

Her stomach dropped. Another body. Aunt Mae would be so disappointed she couldn't spend Christmas with her. With her car out of commission, she'd need to requisition a pool car. She strode back inside the station and filled out the necessary paperwork to get one pool car.

Before now, Pine Grove had a total of two homicides in the last decade. Both were before KC's time, other than the vehicular homicide she handled months ago when she met Tanner. And now, she had her second body in the same week. What was happening to Pine Grove?

The mild December air brushed her skin, and she ducked under the red-and-green striped crime scene tape. Her boots rustled through the dry grass as she approached the lifeless form sprawled near the edge of the park. Despite the holiday lights twinkling in the distance, Florida's lingering warmth clashed with the festive season. The unseasonal humidity added pressure to solve the case quickly before it compromised the evidence.

"What have we got?" She was glad to see Pete.

"Male, mid-thirties." He consulted his notebook. "No ID. Jogger found him about an hour ago."

KC kneeled beside the body, careful not to disturb potential evidence. The man's face was unfamiliar, his clothes nondescript. Nothing about him screamed "local."

The ME van arrived at the same time Morales's

car pulled to a stop. Now why had he shown up? Did he think this was related to Prescott's murder?

A tall woman in an ME jacket got out of the van. She pushed her ponytail over her shoulder and strolled up to KC. "Are you the detective?"

"Yes, KC Cassidy." She extended her hand.

"Luna Hunt from the medical examiner's office." As soon as they shook hands, Hunt gloved up. "What do we have?"

KC pointed to the body where Morales was poking around.

Hunt yelled, "Sir, please don't touch anything. Body is mine."

Morales turned around. "Who are you? Where's Dr. O'Bannon?"

"Luna Hunt, death investigator with the ME office. Dr. O'Bannon doesn't usually go out to the scene. And you are?"

"Detective Frank Morales, sheriff's office."

Hunt proceeded to take charge of the body, squat down, and go about her business.

KC allowed a few minutes to pass before asking, "TOD?"

Hunt pulled out the thermometer, glanced at it, thought for a moment. "Between nine p.m. and three a.m. is my estimate. The ME may revise it after autopsy."

KC nodded.

"Cause of death? Blunt force trauma?" Morales jutted his chin toward the head wound.

The death investigator took her time to examine the body. "Can't say for sure, but here's a bullet wound." She pointed to the back of the body. "No exit wound. The head wound is consistent with being hit by that rock. A possible scenario is he got hit by the bullet, fell, and hit his head. But again, you'll need to wait for Dr. O'Bannon to confirm everything after autopsy."

"You have that contraption to scan his fingerprint?" Morales's gaze lingered on Hunt's bag.

"Patience, Detective." Hunt retrieved a portable fingerprint scanner. A moment later, she raised her eyebrows and got up. "I need to make a quick call to the office."

While Hunt climbed inside the van, Morales crouched by the corpse. "Couldn't she have told us who this was? What's so important that she had to run to call the office?"

"Who knows? Maybe she forgot something important." But KC didn't believe it. More likely, the scan identified someone important. Hunt might want some guidance from her superiors about how to proceed. The dead man wasn't a local celebrity for sure. But could he have been a politician from somewhere?

Once Hunt returned from her phone call, Morales asked again who it was.

"Oh, sorry, it was Tony Beard," Hunt said.

Morales had his pen and notebook out. "Any other details? LKA?"

Hunt shook her head. "Sorry, no last known address and no other details. Excuse me. I need to finish up here. I'll let you know when I'm done so your crime scene guys can do their thing here."

"Let's get out of her way," KC urged Morales.

When KC finished checking out the crime scene and the body in situ after Hunt released it, the sun had long since set. Her phone beeped to alert her of an upcoming appointment.

Tanner.

She surveyed the scene one more time, checked her notes. She had talked to the jogger who found the body. They didn't find any cell phone or wallet or other belongings. The crime scene unit was still combing the area. There was not much she could do now. She would need to run a background check on Tony Beard.

"I bet this case and the Prescott murder are connected." Morales headed to his car.

"Maybe. But I can tell you this Tony Beard wasn't a local."

"Run a background check on him."

"I will once I get back to the station." KC unlocked the car.

"Did the sheriff send you?"

"Nah, I heard it on the radio. Figured I'd come check it out."

KC frowned. Dispatch texted her. How did he know about this?

DECEMBER 24

CHAPTER 14

A half hour later, KC was back home. Tanner arrived sometime after that. Sir Nick, on an extended stay with her, crowded in, glad to see him.

"Have you eaten yet? If not, you're in for a treat. My aunt lives just down the street and is having a feast. I told her I had to work, and she sent over the goodies."

"What are these goodies?" He eyed the containers on the table.

"I'm not sure myself." She opened them one by one. "Cornish hens. Stuffing. Broccoli and cheese. Oh, a quarter of an apple pie."

"Whoa!" He took off his suit jacket and sat at the table. "Looks delicious."

She brought out plates and utensils. While they

ate, she updated him on the latest body. She took a sip of her beer. "Sorry, this isn't quite dinner conversation."

"Ha. Our job doesn't give us a lot of entertaining stories."

"Anyway, I don't know if this guy—" KC's phone beeped with an email. "Excuse me." She tapped it. "The name is an alias. The Tony Beard who fit his description has been dead for over twenty years."

Tanner's hand stopped in midair. "Tony Beard?"

"Yes, did I not say that earlier?"

He put his fork down, leaving the last piece of hen on the plate. "He was an undercover DEA agent. He went dark over two days ago. Now, we know why."

She felt her pulse quicken. "DEA? Was he a member of the op?"

"Yeah." He sighed. "They're not going to like this." He pulled out his phone and started tapping on it.

Minutes later, they set aside their dishes and drank coffee. KC retrieved her laptop and put it on the table. "Before you got here, I did some more research. I've been going over everything — Prescott's murder, Aiden's warning, the second body, the recent incidents—and I'm starting to see a pattern."

He gripped his knees. "Go on."

"Your op is right. There's corruption. Big time. Not just isolated incidents. I think I'm looking at a network, and it might involve some of our own."

She opened her laptop, logged in, and turned it around to show him. "Look at these incident reports. The timing, the locations—they're too convenient. And then there's the matter of evidence going missing from the locker."

Squeezing his knees, he leaned in and scanned the reports. "I see what you mean, but it's circumstantial at best."

"I know, but there's more. I found Tony Beard too. I hope the suspicious transactions have been logged into evidence. Those transactions linked back to a couple of our deputies and people at City Hall."

"It's standard procedure to log in those transactions as evidence."

Wait. Aiden told her about his new gig. "Aiden was doing some work at City Hall. Construction. He's a carpenter. I wonder if he found something while he was there."

"I can't say, but if he did find something, and he

reported it, then he would be in protective custody. In fact, I can confirm that he is."

"When I went to his apartment the other day, it was ransacked."

"They probably know that, but I'll relay it just in case. He warned about a mole. Any idea who that could be?"

She hesitated. "Not really."

He flexed his hands. Must be tension mannerism. "But you have suspicions?"

Sir Nick's toenails clicked on her tile kitchen floor. After slinking closer, he nosed her hand.

"Morales. I get this strange vibe from him." She stroked Sir Nick's neck. "Johnson. He was on duty when the evidence went missing."

"I'll do a deep dive on them and let you know."

"Thanks." Her phone buzzed. She glanced at it and sucked in a breath.

"What is it?" he asked.

She turned the phone so he could see the message.

UNKNOWN NUMBER

Third body. Ticktock, Detective.

He tapped his phone, standing up. "Deanna should get an alert, and I'll let you know what she finds out. And I should be going." He stooped to say goodbye to Sir Nick. "Will you thank your aunt for me? It was delicious. She must be a great cook."

She closed her laptop and got up. "Thanks. She is, and she'll be happy to hear that."

Her phone buzzed again. This time, it was from the dispatcher.

"They found the body. I have to go."

DECEMBER 24

CHAPTER 15

KC stepped out of her unmarked car. Gravel crunched under her boots. The abandoned warehouse loomed before her, its dilapidated frame a stark silhouette against the midnight sky. Red and blue lights from the single patrol car sliced through the darkness, casting eerie shadows across the crumbling walls. There was the familiar ME van, and the Crime Scene Unit was just pulling in.

She approached the entrance. The acrid smell of death hit her as soon as she stepped inside. She'd never get used to it. Under the bright lights, she had to close her eyes for a moment. In the middle, Luna Hunt, the same death investigator, crouched beside the body. Deputy Ramirez stood a good distance away.

"What have we got?" KC craned over Hunt's shoulder. The body was face down. It was a woman with dark hair, professionally dressed.

Hunt looked up. "Female, mid-thirties. Gunshot wound to the back of the head, execution-style." She rolled the body face up.

The unseeing eyes struck KC, no matter how many bodies she'd seen. Thank goodness there hadn't been that many. She kneeled beside her, studying the victim's face. Something was familiar about her.

"Found her press badge." Hunt held up an evidence bag. "Sasha Lee. She's—"

"An investigative journalist," KC supplied. "I heard she'd been digging into a big story about the city hall for months."

"Looks like she dug too deep."

KC stood. First, it was the councilman, then an undercover DEA agent, and now a journalist. She needed to solve this before somebody else died.

"Time of death?" KC asked.

"Preliminary estimate, between six and ten tonight. Will know more after the autopsy."

"Any other evidence?"

"Crime scene just got here. I'm done." Hunt pushed to her feet and motioned for the technicians to take the body. "The scene is yours. Um, just want to point something out to you."

Hunt led KC to a far corner. There, bright-red spray paint left a chilling message:

SILENCE IS GOLDEN

Shivers ran down her spine. The killer wasn't just silencing a journalist. They were sending a warning. She thanked Hunt who nodded and turned to leave.

Leaving crime scene technicians to do their jobs, she went back to Ramirez. "Who found her?"

"Two teenagers who were looking for some thrills. They're in the patrol car now."

She raised an eyebrow, and he smirked. "A boy and a girl."

Ah! An abandoned warehouse? Can't the guy be more romantic? KC strolled toward the patrol unit. The girl looked shell-shocked. The boy wore a stoic expression under his Orlando Magic cap.

"Can I see some IDs?" She opened the back door.

The boy fumbled in his pocket for his wallet, and the girl, upon nudging by her boyfriend, got hers out of her little purse. Jace Burton, aged eighteen, and Madison Sommers, aged eighteen as well. They were probably high school seniors.

KC asked them to recount their stories. They came to have a little fun, but before anything happened, Madison saw the body and screamed.

"Nobody was here. I didn't see any car," Jace finished. "But someone might have snuck away."

"What made you say that?"

"I heard noises. Leaves crunching underfoot, like he was running away. Maybe his car was parked somewhere else."

Wow. What kid has the presence of mind to notice these things?

Before she asked, he shrugged. "I'm in the police explorer program. I learn to pay attention to details at a crime scene."

KC gave him another look. Jace had to be referring to the program the Orlando PD offered.

"Good job. Anything else?"

When Madison shook her head, Jace pointed to the back of the warehouse. "I think he went that way. But that's it."

"Okay, thanks." KC would make sure CSU searched that area. After ensuring Ramirez had their contact information, she released them.

"Hey, Cassidy!" Morales waved and jogged over.

Why was he here? He was dressed in a black jogging outfit.

It's after midnight!

Not her business.

"What'd I miss?" His hands hooked to his waist as he craned around.

She updated him.

"Hmm... given the victim's profession, this case will get some attention."

"I know. I'm gonna start with her office, colleagues, the usual."

"Let me handle that. Why don't you check out what she's been researching recently."

"Sure, I'll do that. But I'll talk to her editor."

KC made another round of the scene and walked to her car. She drove back to the station, her mind racing with possibilities and connections. At her desk, she jotted down some notes for the coming day. Interview Sasha Lee's editor. Review warehouse ownership records—why did Lee go there?

Exhausted but wired, KC headed home for a couple of hours of restless sleep.

DECEMBER 25

CHAPTER 16

The next morning, KC made it to the church just as the service was starting. Normally, she'd have gone to the midnight service with her aunt, but criminals didn't care about holidays. After the service, KC called the *Pine Grove Gazette*, the newspaper where Lee worked. She was betting they would stay open to cover this developing story, especially since the victim was one of their own. She was right.

"Detective Cassidy," Greg Parsons, Lee's editor, greeted her with a somber expression. "I still can't believe it."

"I'm sorry for your loss." KC sat. "I need to know what Sasha was working on."

Parsons's lips pursed, and his brows furrowed.

"Listen, Sasha was a friend. I want to help. However, I'm afraid I can't tell you that. We need to protect our sources."

She narrowed her eyes. "Even to protect Sasha's killer?"

He sighed. "I can only tell you that she'd been working on this for months. If you read her work, you should have an idea of what she is—was—about." His fingers kept tapping an opened file on his desk. And then he stood up. "Excuse me. I need to check something."

KC took the hint. She got up and peered at the open file. The words were tiny, so she took a picture for later. But the photo was easily recognizable. Victor Holloway. Whatever Lee was investigating was related to Holloway, the mayor's chief of staff.

She left the office and talked to several of Lee's coworkers. None had anything significant to contribute. Nobody knew what she was working on. Just that it was juicy and big. Given the holiday, she found the office abuzz. The mood was somber, but the journalists all wanted her to keep them updated.

Now that she knew about Holloway, she needed to arm herself with some knowledge before confronting him.

Back at the station, she dove into Lee's recent articles. A pattern emerged: shell companies making large donations to local campaigns, including the late councilman's.

Her phone buzzed with a text.

UNKNOWN NUMBER

> Digging deep? Be careful where you step.

KC's jaw clenched. She forwarded the message to Tanner, then refocused on her work.

By midafternoon, she had a breakthrough. One of the shell companies, Gulfstream Investments, had recently purchased a property. Almost holding her breath, she pulled up the address— it matched the warehouse where Lee's body was found.

She was about to dig deeper when Morales appeared at her desk.

"Cassidy, did you find anything?"

KC hesitated. "Following a few leads. Nothing solid yet. What are you doing here? It's Christmas."

"Merry Christmas to you too! Just checking in is all." He did a mock salute and left.

Cyber investigations absorbed her. Before she realized it, it was time to meet Tanner. Instead of her house, she headed to a twenty-four-hour diner, the only one in town that stayed open year-round. Tanner stood out from the few men there.

"One year, when we had a case during the holiday, we had a feast in the office to celebrate." Tanner said by way of greeting.

"Normally, I celebrate with my aunt. This is the first year I've had to work—there are now three dead bodies, by the way. So, what have you got?"

He leaned in. "Our tech confirmed it. Your car was tampered with. Brake line was cut."

"Geez." She paused when a waitress stopped by to give them coffee and take their orders.

When would anyone have a chance? It had to be between her arrival at and departure from the station. Few people had been around the station. She told him as much.

Tanner had his mug in his hand. "They're checking security footage."

KC filled him in on her day's findings. "This goes deep. Holloway, the shell companies, the warehouse—it's all connected. And now someone's trying to scare me off the case. Did your tech find out about who keeps texting me?"

"Deanna is trying. Apparently, the sophisticated bouncing techniques they're using make it hard to pinpoint."

"So we're dealing with professionals."

"Looks that way. Now, your turn."

She took a deep breath. "The body. Sasha Lee."

His eyebrows shot up. "The journalist?"

"Execution-style. And there was a message at the scene. 'Silence is golden.'"

Tanner cursed under his breath. "This is escalating fast."

His grilled chicken and her tuna salad sandwiches arrived. They dug in.

"It gets worse. I've been digging into Lee's recent articles. She was investigating a series of shell companies—all linked to large donations to local political campaigns."

"The same shell companies connected to Prescott's campaign?"

"Exactly. And guess whose name keeps popping up? Victor Holloway. He's the mayor's chief of staff." She checked her sandwich. It was Christmas, and she was eating a tuna salad sandwich.

"Wow! The plot thickens." He devoured almost half of his chicken already.

"One of these shell companies made a large purchase recently. A warehouse on the outskirts of town." She tested her sandwich. At least, the diner did make *the best* tuna salad.

"Let me guess. The same warehouse where you found Lee's body."

"Ding, ding, ding! We have a winner. Lee must've been close to exposing something big."

"Big enough to kill for."

"I need to get into that warehouse again. What if I missed something?"

Tanner put his fork down. "Too risky. If Holloway is involved, you can bet that place is being watched. Did your CSU find anything?"

"Not much. The perp policed his brass. No shell casings anywhere." She told him about Jace. "The kid was right. They followed the tracks leading away. But the only thing they found was a zipper pull."

"A zipper pull? What kind?"

"Regular kind. Not round, but square. Unless there's blood or some other DNA on it, it's basically useless."

KC's phone buzzed. She glanced at it, went lightheaded. "Another body?"

She turned the phone so he could see another text.

> UNKNOWN NUMBER
>
> Curiosity killed the cat. And the journalist. Ticktock, Detective.

"Now, he's just taunting. He's getting confident. Overconfident. This is when he'll—"

"Make a mistake." She finished it for him with

a smile.

DECEMBER 25

CHAPTER 17

The moment KC paid her check, Tanner's cell chimed. He pulled it out, glanced at it, and raised his gaze. "Something is going down at the old warehouse."

Without waiting for more, KC went to her loaner. Soon, the building loomed before her. She parked and approached, one hand on her holstered weapon. Tanner still hadn't arrived. Maybe he'd gotten lost.

Nope, he pulled in now. He stepped out, a USB drive in his hand. "I picked it up from my contact. You were so eager to get out of Dodge that you missed meeting Olivia."

"Who's she?"

"You can say she's a consultant for the task force."

"And what's in this?" She gestured toward the USB drive. "And why are we here?"

"Financial records. They implicate Deputy Johnson in a major way." He secured the drive back in his pocket. "He's been laundering money for the drug operation through his brother's construction company. And because he's around here somewhere."

She unholstered her weapon and kept her hand there. Johnson was on her list. His financials looked suspicious, but she couldn't dig too deeply without a warrant or alerting anyone. They cautiously went inside the warehouse. "Are you sure?"

"It's all here. Account numbers, dates, amounts." He pulled his gun out.

She heard it too and drew her weapon.

The warehouse door creaked open. She and Tanner were ready.

"Detective Cassidy? Is that you?"

It was Johnson.

KC and Tanner exchanged a look. How much had he heard? There was no hiding. "Yeah, Johnson."

Deputy Johnson rounded the corner, his hand

resting casually on his holster. His eyes narrowed as he took in the scene.

"Sir, I need you to put your weapon down." Johnson pointed his gun at Tanner.

"Stand down, Johnson," KC commanded. "This is Special Agent Nathan Tanner, FBI."

Johnson darted his gaze between KC and Tanner, lowering his gun. "What's going on?"

"I asked to meet with the detective here about a classified case." Tanner kept his weapon at the ready.

Before Johnson said anything, KC asked, "What are you doing here? It's out of your patrol area."

"Dispatch said you were headed this way. Thought you might need backup."

Tanner threw her a glance to tell her it was a lie. KC knew that and stiffened under the tension. It only took a moment before Johnson realized something was wrong. His hand tightened on his weapon.

"Johnson, let's talk."

It happened in an instant. Johnson raised his gun, but Tanner was faster. His shot caught Johnson in the shoulder, sending him stumbling backward.

"Cuff him!" Tanner hollered.

But Johnson wasn't done. With a grunt, he scrambled to his feet and bolted for the exit.

Tanner cursed, and KC gave chase. They burst out of the warehouse into the cool December air. Johnson was already halfway across the parking lot, headed for his patrol car.

KC's feet pounded the pavement as she sprinted after him. "Johnson, stop! Don't make this worse!"

But Johnson was beyond reason. He threw himself into his vehicle and gunned the engine.

KC skidded to a stop by the pool car, Tanner already hopped into the passenger seat. She jumped behind the wheel.

The evening exploded into a cacophony of sirens and screeching tires as she tore after Johnson. The quiet small-town streets blurred as they raced through intersections, narrowly avoiding the rush of last-minute shoppers.

"This is Detective Cassidy," KC said into her radio. "I'm in pursuit of Deputy Johnson, heading east on Main Street. Suspect is armed and dangerous. Set up roadblocks on all major exits."

Johnson's patrol car fishtailed as he hooked a sharp turn onto a narrow side street. KC followed, her knuckles white on the steering wheel.

"Give it up, Johnson!" she shouted, though he couldn't hear her. "There's nowhere to run!"

The chase led them to the outskirts where the

paved roads gave way to gravel. Johnson's car kicked up a cloud of dust, obscuring her vision.

"Watch out!" Tanner hollered.

Then Johnson's brake lights flared.

KC barely had time to react as his car skidded sideways and blocked the road. She slammed on her brakes, her car coming to a stop inches from Johnson's.

Before she could catch her breath, Johnson was out of his vehicle, gun in hand.

KC and Tanner ducked. A bullet shattered her windshield. Glass rained around them as she rolled out of the car and took cover behind the open door.

"Johnson, don't be stupid!" she yelled. "Put the gun down!"

Another shot rang out, pinging off her hood.

"You don't understand!" Johnson shouted back, his voice cracking. "They'll kill my family if I talk!"

"This is a federal case." Tanner hollered, "We can protect them, Johnson! But you need to surrender!"

Silence fell.

KC held her breath, straining to hear any movement.

Then Johnson's voice came again, softer this

time. "I'm sorry, Detective. I didn't want any of this."

KC risked a glance around the car door. Johnson stood in the open, his gun hanging limply at his side. The fight had gone out of him.

She stood, keeping her weapon trained on Johnson. "Put the gun down."

Tanner went over and grabbed the weapon from Johnson's hand.

KC cuffed Johnson and sirens neared.

"Talk to me, Johnson." She secured his hands behind his back. "Who's behind all this?"

He shook his head. A trembling started in his arms. "I can't. They're everywhere, Detective. City Hall, the business community... it goes all the way up."

Before KC could press for more details, a fleet of patrol cars arrived, lights flashing. Tanner whispered to her, "Here, I have a copy." He slipped her the drive. "I need to scoot. Will bring the car back to you. You can get a ride home."

He got into her pool car and drove off.

It's not my car!

Morales came over. "What happened?"

Why was he here? Why did he keep responding to her substation's call?

"Johnson has been laundering money."

"Really?"

"Yeah, I have proof." She touched the drive in her pocket.

She hitched a ride back to the station and debated doing the paperwork later. Johnson was processed and led into a cell. She wanted to talk to him before he lawyered up. Maybe he would tell her who was behind it all.

"Detective!" Pete burst into the room. "You need to come quick. It's Johnson."

KC rushed to the cell.

Johnson lay on the floor, his body convulsing, foam bubbling from his mouth.

"No, no, no," she muttered as she fumbled with the keys. "Get a medic in here now!"

But even as they rushed to Johnson's side, KC knew it was too late. His eyes, wide with terror, locked onto hers before the light faded from them.

As the chaos of emergency response swirled around her, KC stood rooted to the spot, her mind reeling. Johnson had been silenced before he could talk.

Who had access to him? He was in their custody. Morales. She prayed the autopsy would give her a clue to find out how the poison was administered.

DECEMBER 26

CHAPTER 18

The next day in Pine Grove dawned warm and humid, a typical December day in Florida. The weather sure was a far cry from the snowy Christmas scenes depicted on greeting cards. But the residents of this close-knit community were accustomed to celebrating the holiday season with a subtropical twist. Twinkling lights adorned palm trees, and the scent of blooming jasmine mingled with the festive spirit.

KC wiped sweat from her brow as she pushed open the doors to the medical examiner's office. The blast of cold air from the building's overworked AC unit was a sharp contrast to the muggy heat outside. Instead of the aroma of roasting turkey, she found herself surrounded by the sterile scent of disinfectant.

Like her, Dr. O'Bannon apparently had come in early to catch up on work. Now, he looked up from his desk. His grave expression said this wouldn't be a quick visit.

"Detective." He stood, gestured for her to follow him into the autopsy room. "I had a feeling you'd be by this morning."

She steeled herself for what she was about to see. On the cold metal table lay the body of Deputy Johnson, his skin pale under the harsh fluorescent lights. A chill traced down KC's spine, a stark reminder of the danger now lurking in their small town.

"I've completed the preliminary examination." Dr. O'Bannon picked up a clipboard, his voice taking on a professional tone. "We're still waiting on the full tox screen, but I'm confident in my initial findings."

He moved to the side of the table and pointed to a small, almost imperceptible mark on Johnson's thigh. "See this? Injection site. Based on the symptoms reported and the preliminary tests, I believe cyanide was introduced into Deputy Johnson's system through this point."

KC leaned in, her eyes narrowing as she examined the tiny puncture. "Cyanide? That's not exactly an easy substance to come by."

"No, it's not. But that's the cause of death. Manner would be homicide."

Was there a scuffle last night? She thought he'd given up. She'd have to ask the deputies who had secured Johnson.

"I'll have the full report for you as soon as the tox screen comes back." The doc removed his gloves with a snap.

"Thanks, Doc."

As she left the morgue, she breathed deeply, her mind shifting gears to her next moves. Someone had killed Deputy Johnson to prevent him from talking. She needed to find out who. Too close to give up now.

The fluorescent lights of the Pine Grove substation buzzed incessantly as she made a quick stop to update the case board. She pinned up a note about the cyanide injection, but her gaze lingered on a sealed envelope on her desk—the long-awaited list of buyers for the special-edition cuff link. That list could unravel the whole conspiracy, including the first three murders.

She frowned at the wall clock. *How is it almost noon already?* She pulled out her phone and sent Tanner a quick, encrypted message.

> KC
> New development. Johnson, cyanide injection. Homicide confirmed. We need to talk ASAP.

The door swung open. Off guard, she almost dropped her phone.

Sheriff Hawkins strode in, his features taut. "KC, we need to talk."

She stood and gestured for him to take a seat.

He did. "The state police are talking about taking over the investigation."

"With all due respect, Sheriff, that would be a mistake. We're too close to—"

"I know, I know," he cut her off, raising a hand. "That's why I'm here. I need you to brief me on everything you've got. No holds barred."

KC took a deep breath. She trusted Hawkins, but there was still the mole.

"Sheriff, what I'm about to tell you... It goes beyond Johnson. Beyond the department. We think the local drug operation might be a front for something much bigger."

His eyebrows shot up. "How much bigger?"

"City hall bigger."

The sheriff let out a low whistle. "That's quite

an accusation, KC. You'd better have some solid evidence."

She gauged his reaction. Unless he was a great poker player, he wasn't in on it. "I've been tracking money movements, shell companies, mysterious 'consultancy' fees. It all points to a sophisticated operation with tendrils reaching into local government."

As KC laid out their findings, his already taut features grew increasingly grim. When she finished, he sat back, rubbing his temples.

"Geez. If even half of this is true..."

A beat later, she scooted her chair in closer. "There's more. I've been working with—"

Her phone buzzed.

TANNER

Urgent. Call ASAP.

"I'm sorry, sir. I need to take this. It's... related to the case."

Hawkins stood up. "I need to hit the head anyway, but we're not done."

Before calling Tanner, KC eyed the sealed envelope containing the cuff link buyers' list. She opened it and scanned the names. Her heart raced as she spotted a familiar name near the top of the list.

She called Tanner, who answered right away. "I've got news. Our tech team finally traced the origin of those texts you've been getting."

"And?"

"They came from someone in City Hall."

A chill ran down her spine. "City Hall? Remember that list of buyers I mentioned? The special edition cuff links? The mayor's chief of staff's name is on it. Are you thinking what I'm thinking?"

"It can't be a coincidence. A good chance he might be your killer and mole. At the very least, he is involved somehow."

Suddenly, Tanner's voice cut off, replaced by a series of beeps. "I've got another call coming in. Hold on a second."

She moved to the case board, willing it to talk to her until he came back on.

"My DEA contact just called." Tension thrummed in his voice. "They intercepted an encrypted call. There's a major shipment moving tonight."

"Where?" KC reached for her jacket.

"The old lumber mill on Route 7."

"We need to move. Now."

"Whoa, hold on," he cautioned. "Let them do their job. We'll just be in their way."

KC clenched a fist. "But I can't sit back and do nothing."

"Why don't you focus on the mayor's chief of staff? He seems to be a solid lead. By the way, did you find out more about Johnson's death?"

The mention of Johnson's name reminded her to update Tanner. She pulled up the notes on the screen. "I did. After he was processed, Deputy Simmons escorted him to the cell. On their way, Morales bumped into him by accident. Supposedly."

"So, either Simmons or Morales could—"

"Not Pete, I mean, Simmons. I trust him. He's my eye and ear in here."

Tanner didn't say anything for a beat. "So, Morales?"

"His name is on my list."

"The zipper pull?"

She sighed. "I don't think..." An image popped into her head. A black jogging outfit. The way his hand was opening...

"What?"

"I just thought of something." Was she imagining it? "Morales showed up at the scene in a jogging outfit. Let me look." She rummaged through her desk and searched in her emails. Finally, the report from the lab. "Here it is. There's a designer tag attached to the pull. And guess what? They found two partial prints, one on each side."

"Any match?"

"Not yet. The quality isn't that great. But they're trying." She spotted the sheriff approaching. "Hey, I gotta go."

"Everything all right?"

"Yes, sir. Just following up on a lead."

Hawkins studied her, then nodded. "Okay, keep me posted. We need this solved."

"Yes, sir."

After moments of deliberation, she called Tanner again to discuss her thoughts.

KC spent the rest of the day diving into Victor Holloway. The man was in the Marines and served as a sniper. He had the skill necessary to pull off the murders of the councilman and the undercover DEA agent. But the journalist? She had someone else in mind for that. Now, she just needed to collect the evidence.

As night fell, KC drove to the old lumber mill and parked a good way away.

"Howdy?"

She jumped at the voice when she got out of the car. It was Tanner. "You scared me."

"Sorry." He smiled. "Let's check it out."

They crept closer, using the overgrown foliage

as cover. Voices carried on the night air, and KC strained to make out the words.

"...final shipment before we shut down the operation," a gruff voice was saying. "The boss wants everything cleared out by dawn."

KC and Tanner exchanged a look. This was it—the evidence.

A twig snapped under KC's foot. The voices stopped.

"What was that?"

KC froze. Tanner skulked away.

A beam of light cut through the darkness, sweeping closer to her hiding spot.

DECEMBER 26

CHAPTER 19

The beam of light inched closer, threatening to expose KC's position. Her hand tightened on her weapon, adrenaline surging through her veins. Where had Tanner gone? He couldn't have left her, but she pushed the thought aside. She had to focus on the present.

"Police! Drop your weapons!" she called, hoping to catch their pursuers off guard.

More gunshots. She ducked behind a large oak, her breath coming in ragged gasps. She peered around the trunk, trying to get a bead on their attackers.

In the chaos, she glimpsed men in dark clothing, their faces obscured. One figure stood out—the leader. His form looked familiar.

"Don't let her escape!"

She knew that voice. Before she could process the implications, a bullet whizzed past her ear. She returned fire; her shot finding its mark. A cry of pain confirmed that.

No way would she leave empty-handed. She wanted proof of the corruption that ensnared Pine Grove.

Engines roared.

She cursed under her breath. They weren't getting away, not on her watch. A plan formed. It was risky, but it was her only shot.

KC darted toward the lumber mill, laying down suppressing fire as she moved. In the distance, sirens wailed—someone had called the cops.

The familiar voice—Morales's—cursed. "Pack it up! Now!"

Several large trucks were being hastily loaded. This was how they were moving their product—hiding drugs and other illicit goods among legitimate lumber shipments. A clever scheme, using the town's dying industry as a cover.

A blow to the back of her head sent her sprawling. Stars exploded in her vision as she hit the ground hard.

"Well, well," Morales drawled. "I knew you wouldn't quit. I tried to steer you away from the investigations, but you just wouldn't stop. You're just too stubborn. Ignored our warnings."

Her vision swam as someone hauled her to her feet. She stood face-to-face with Morales. But he'd said, "we." So, he wasn't the mastermind. She didn't think so anyway.

His grip on her arm tightened.

"Why, Morales? How long have you been part of this?"

"Part of this?" He laughed. "I prefer to think of it as... a

necessary evil. This town was dying. We helped give it a new purpose."

"Pine Grove may be a small town, but it isn't dying." She ground her teeth and glared. "And how are you helping? By turning it into a drug-trafficking hub?"

"Among other things. You'd be amazed by what people will ship when they think no one's looking. But you're only seeing a small part of the picture."

Sirens grew louder.

Morales's expression hardened. "All right, change of plans. You're coming with us."

They shoved her toward a waiting van. Its engine roared to life, tires squealing as it peeled away from the ancient lumber mill. She sat on the floor, hands zip-tied behind her back, Morales's gun trained on her.

"You won't get away with this," she warned. *Where are you, Tanner?*

Morales smirked. "I already have. By the time anyone figures out what's happening, we'll be long gone."

"The sheriff—"

"Is an idiot. He never suspected a thing. It was almost too easy."

"You're making a mistake. Others know about this operation. They'll be all over this place before you know it."

Morales swallowed hard enough to bob his Adam's apple. Then he raised his chin. "Then I guess we'll have to speed things up."

He turned to the driver. "Change of plans. Take us to the backup site."

The van swerved a sharp turn.

She had to act fast. "It was you, wasn't it?" Well, act fast and stall. "You killed Johnson."

"He was going to talk. We can't have that."

"And the journalist?"

"Loose ends." He shrugged. "This business requires a certain... ruthlessness."

"How many more, Morales? How many people have to die for your 'business'?"

"As many as it takes. But you're barking up the wrong tree. I'm not the one calling all the shots here."

Now they were getting somewhere. Who was behind all this? "So, you're not the top dog."

"Top dog? Nah, I'm just a *cog* in a much larger machine. Let's just say this operation goes higher up than you could imagine."

The van jolted to a stop, an abandoned warehouse beyond the rear window.

"End of the line." Morales gestured with his gun. "Out."

They marched into the warehouse. KC scanned the mostly empty interior, the old crates and rusted machinery.

Morales forced her to her knees, his gun never wavering. "I want names," he demanded. "Who else knows about our operation?"

Silence.

"Have it your way." He raised his gun.

"Drop your weapon!" Tanner stepped forward with a gun trained on Morales, then turned to KC. "Sorry, I had to make sure backup didn't get lost."

KC smiled. Tanner came through. Their plan had worked.

Ruddy hues blotched Morales's face. "You're bluffing."

"Wanna bet?"

His gun hand wavered.

KC launched herself, bound hands and all, at Morales and tackled him to the ground.

Chaos erupted. She fought, handicapped by her bound hands but driven by sheer determination.

A gunshot rang out. Pain seared her side, but she kept fighting. Then she got her hands on a piece of broken machinery and used it to cut through her zip ties.

"KC!" Tanner tossed her his backup weapon.

She snatched it up just as Morales regained his footing. For a heartbeat, they faced each other, guns raised.

"It's over, Morales." KC panted, ignoring the blood seeping through her shirt. "Drop the weapon."

Morales's gaze darted between her and Tanner.

DEA and FBI agents swooped in, their guns out. "Drop your weapon!" someone hollered.

"Hands behind your head!" another agent commanded.

Morales cursed and lowered his gun. "You've got nothing. No evidence, no witnesses. It's your word against mine."

"That's where you're wrong." She nodded toward the shadows.

A figure stepped into view. Sheriff Tom Hawkins emerged, holding up his phone.

"We got it all," Hawkins said, his voice heavy with disappointment. "Every single word."

KC pulled out the wire she was wearing and showed Morales. "Technology comes in handy." The adrenaline rush faded, and the pain intensified. She swayed on her feet.

Tanner rushed to her and pressed down on her wound. "We need an ambulance right now!" he said to whoever was on the other end of his earbud. And he turned back to her. "Hey, stay with me, KC. It's over. We did it."

Darkness crept into the edges of her vision, and she struggled to stay focused. "Yeah..."

DECEMBER 28

CHAPTER 20

KC first became aware of the steady beep of a heart monitor, then the noises around her. People talking. She tried to open her eyes, but her eyelids seemed so heavy.

"Kylie, I know you can hear me. Nate came by a few times. He seems like a keeper. Once you're up and about, we should invite him over for dinner."

Oh no! Nobody called her Kylie except for Aunt Mae. She better not have said anything to Tanner to embarrass her. She heard footsteps. Someone just walked in. With great effort, KC opened her eyes. She blinked, her vision slowly focusing on a sterile white ceiling. A dull ache in her side reminded her of the bullet wound she'd sustained.

"Welcome back, sleeping beauty," a familiar voice said.

Tanner came into her vision. He stood beside Aunt Mae, who was seated by her bed. KC looked from one to the other.

"Oh, honey." Aunt Mae touched her hand. "We met already."

Her aunt always had the ability to read her mind.

"How... how long was I out?" KC croaked, her throat dry.

"About thirty-six hours." Tanner offered her a glass of water. "You had us worried there for a bit."

Aunt Mae held the straw to her mouth.

As KC sipped the water, the door opened. Sheriff Hawkins entered, followed by a lanky black man and a woman.

"Good to see you awake, KC." Hawkins grinned. "How are you feeling?"

"Like I've been shot," she quipped. "But I'll live. What's the situation?"

"I guess she's back to normal!" Aunt Mae stood up. "I need to use the restroom and get something to drink. I'll be back, dear."

The men nodded, and parted the way to let her aunt walk out.

The black guy stepped forward. "Detective Cassidy, I'm Special Agent Jake Cooper, DEA. And this is Special Agent Lia Blake, FBI. Are you well enough to talk? If not, we can come back."

KC searched for the button to raise the head of the bed, wincing at the pain. Tanner pressed the button for her and handed her the control.

"Thanks. And yes, I'm good." She blinked a few times, hoping to revive her memories. "Before we do that, my memories are a bit hazy. Can someone remind me what happened? I mean, Morales took me to the warehouse."

Tanner frowned. "Do you remember me and the sheriff showing up?"

"Yeah, but how?"

Hawkins and Tanner exchange glances. Then Tanner said, "Your sheriff has been working for the joint op. He had to play dumb to flush out the mole. Morales took the bait. When I slipped away, I called Sheriff Hawkins, and he arranged for the backup. I don't know if you remember, but you and I had the plan to get Morales to incriminate himself. But when he threatened to shoot you, I had to intervene."

Hawkins smiled. "He never suspected me."

She looked from one to the other. "I'd never have guessed you were with the joint op." She then turned her gaze toward Cooper and Blake. "All right, lay it on me."

"Okay then, but first, let me commend you on your exceptional work." Blake smiled. "Thanks to your efforts, we've unraveled a criminal network that spans far beyond Pine Grove."

"Morales?"

"In custody," Hawkins confirmed. "He took the deal. Sang like a songbird."

Cooper had a tight smile on. "According to the Assistant US Attorney, we still need more evidence to substantiate his claim, in particular, the mayor."

"Mayor Hutchins?" During the interview, Hutchins hadn't liked her questions about the rejected projects.

"Yeah," Blake said. "But we'll get the evidence. We're checking all communication and financial records. We'll find something. And we haven't questioned her chief of staff yet. He might roll too."

"Victor Holloway?"

"Yup. We, er, actually you did it. The cuff link. We traced it to him. And door cam footage down the street from the councilman's house shows him going to his house and leaving about ten minutes later." Blake showed KC the footage on her tablet.

Cooper added, "I'm confident he's also responsible for our undercover agent's death. We executed a sneak-and-peek and hit pay dirt. Found a sniper's rifle. We're waiting on the ballistic match."

KC didn't have the energy to celebrate, even though she wanted to. All she could do was offer a weak smile. "Did you seize any drugs and assets?"

The DEA agent grinned. "Over fifty million in drugs and assets. And that's just the tip of the iceberg."

Tanner touched her hand. "You did good. Morales copped to the journalist's murder. And to swiping evidence."

"Did he mess with my car?"

"No, that was Johnson, but the order came from Holloway. You got too close."

"I knew I was"—she paused to take a breath—"on the right track."

"Why don't you rest now?" Tanner stood.

The door opened, and Aunt Mae looked surprised to see they were still there.

"We're just leaving, Mrs. Reeves." Hawkins patted KC's hand.

Cooper and Blake nodded their goodbyes and walked out. KC grabbed Tanner's hand. "Can you find out about Aiden? It hit me that the undercover agent might be the one who drove Aiden away."

He squeezed her hand. "I'll see what I find out."

The next day, KC was itching to sit up and get out of the hospital. But of course, the doctors and Aunt Mae wouldn't hear of it. So, she watched mindless TV to pass the time. Her injury wasn't severe. The bullet didn't hit any major arteries or organs. It hurt, but she'd get over it. One more day and she would leave —at least, that's what she told herself.

"Hey, KC." Tanner entered the hospital room. "How are you feeling?"

She shifted in her bed, wincing slightly at the pain in her side. "Better and bored. Any news?"

He pulled up a chair and sat. "Actually, yes. I found out something about Aiden."

"Is he okay?"

"He's fine. Like I told you, he's in protective custody."

She frowned. "Yeah, I remember now. I wonder why he didn't tell me."

"He's not allowed to divulge any information. That's to protect him. But now that the case seems to be wrapping up, I'm sure he'll be back soon."

"I wonder how he got to be a witness. Do you

think he saw someone kill the councilman? No, it can't be. He was already gone by then."

"From what I heard, he has information about the money-laundering scheme and drug operation."

Mundane announcements crackled the hospital PA system as she ran over things in her head. "Now it makes sense. He had a gig at the city hall. I bet he heard or saw something. Then he somehow connected with the DEA or the FBI. That's why he warned me about a mole."

Tanner gripped his knees. "Sounds about right. Your councilman was investigating irregularities in the town's finances, shell companies, unusual patterns in local businesses."

"But I remember some weird deposits in his account."

"They tried to buy him. And when that didn't work, they left the money there to implicate him. I guess he must have confronted them and they had to get rid of him."

Her mouth opened to an *O*. "That's why Pete saw him arguing with someone and a squad car picked up the guy he was arguing with. I bet that was when he threatened to expose them and they took him out."

"Like they tried to do with you." He squeezed his knees again. "By the way, they arrested Holloway and offered him a deal to roll on the mayor. He'd still get life without parole, just not the needle."

KC leaned back, overwhelmed. "I can't believe it. All this time..."

"You should be proud. Your persistence, your refusal to let this go—it brought down this entire operation. You're a hero, Detective Cassidy."

"I'm no hero. I was just doing my job." Just about a week ago, KC thought Pine Grove was nothing like a big city. Policing was mundane. And now, she cracked the town's biggest corruption case. Not to mention she helped the DEA and the FBI take down the drug operation and money-laundering scheme.

"Let's see if they arrested the mayor yet." Tanner turned on the TV.

DECEMBER 30

CHAPTER 21

A festive atmosphere permeated the Pine Grove station, despite the lack of any chill in the December air. A colorful banner hung across the bullpen, its cheerful letters proclaiming, "Welcome Back, Detective Cassidy!" It was two days before New Year's Day, and the station buzzed with a mix of holiday cheer.

KC pushed open the glass doors. She paused, taking in the banner and the twinkling lights strung around the reception desk. A smile claimed her lips as she stepped inside, the familiar scent of stale coffee and paper files welcoming her back.

"Well, well, look who's back early!" Pete raised his mug in salute. "Couldn't stay away, could you, KC?"

She chuckled and shrugged off her jacket. "What can I say? Daytime TV gets old fast."

KC made her way to her office and met a chorus of welcome backs and good-natured ribbing about her early return. She grimaced as she settled into her chair.

"Cassidy, good to have you back!" Sheriff Hawkins walked in.

"Thanks!" She started to stand.

"No." He motioned for her to stay seated and sat across from her. "How are you feeling? You know you didn't have to come back until after the holidays."

"I'm fine, Sheriff. Just a bit sore still. Honestly, I was going stir-crazy at home. There's only so much TV a person can watch."

He chuckled, then leaned forward. "Listen, KC, I need to talk to you about something." He paused. "I saw your transfer request."

Her heart pounded. This was when he came to tell her the bad news.

"I don't have any openings at the main office right now. But the Orlando PD is looking for a detective. If you're interested, the job is yours. Well, I kind of pulled some strings."

She couldn't speak for a moment. Stunned. "I thought the mayor's nephew—"

"Oh yes. I finally got the funding for one more detective here."

Oh, she'd been worrying for nothing!

"I'll be honest," Hawkins continued, "I'd be sad to lose you. But I want you to be happy. I want you somewhere you can flourish, use all that talent of yours. And if that's not here in Pine Grove... well, then I want to help you find where it is."

A lump formed in her throat. KC swallowed hard. Orlando... Hmm... She'd be right where Tanner worked. "Thank you, sir. Can I think about it?"

"Of course." He stood up. "Just don't take too long."

She stood and extended her hand. "Thank you, Sheriff. For everything."

Hawkins shook her hand. "You've earned it, KC."

The rest of the day passed in a blur of catch-up work and festive interruptions. As the afternoon waned, KC stared at her phone, her aunt's number on the screen. With a deep breath, she hit the call button.

"Hi, Aunt Mae, about that dinner... is that offer to bring someone still open?"

Later that evening, as KC locked up her desk,

she pulled out her phone again. Her finger hovered over Tanner's number before she pressed call.

"Tanner, I was wondering... My aunt's having a big dinner to make up for my missing out on Christmas dinner, and well... would you like to come?"

Buried Secrets - Where It All Begins, the first gripping installment in the Mirror Estate series, is available on Amazon and Kindle Unlimited. Grab it now, or any other Mirror Estate Series book to learn more about Nathan Tanner and Task Force 629.

THANK YOU!

Thank you for diving into *Christmas Murders*! Writing this story has been such a wild ride and knowing that you've spent time with KC and the world Pine Grove means the world to me.

    I hope you loved reading it as much as I loved writing it. If you'd be so kind as to leave a review on Amazon and/or Goodreads to share your impressions with others, I would greatly appreciate it. Your insights will help other readers find the book.

BURIED SECRETS – WHERE IT ALL BEGINS

A SUSPENSE THRILLER

BOOK 1 OF MIRROR ESTATE SERIES

SNEAK PEEK

32 YEARS AGO

"Took care of the cop."

"Good. Found the evidence?"

There was a pause. "Not yet. Not anywhere in his house."

"Find it!"

No more needed to be said. They knew what was at stake.

CHAPTER 1

FINAL GOODBYE

SEATTLE

Dylan Roche didn't recognize half the people shaking his hand, and the ones he did spoke in hushed voices, careful not to say too much. He nodded, numb, as water dripped from the cemetery's oaks onto the mourners below. His black suit —borrowed from Tommy—fit well enough, though the sleeves hung a little too long.

After the final prayer, Fr. Jon approached. "Your mother always made time for Adoration before her shifts, even if it was just fifteen minutes. I believe her faith shone in a special way. You might be surprised how many lives she touched by being there."

"She was a wonderful woman." Mrs. Patterson

from the apartment next door shook his hand. "Always so quiet, so polite."

Dylan nodded. "Thank you for coming."

"Dylan." Tommy appeared at his elbow as the last mourners drifted toward their cars. "You holding up okay?"

"Yeah." The word came out hoarse. Dylan cleared his throat. "Thanks for being here."

"Where else would I be?" Tommy straightened his tie. "Listen, my folks wanted me to tell you again, anything you need, just let us know. Mom's already made three casseroles for your freezer."

Dylan managed a smile. "Tell her I appreciate it."

They walked toward the parking area, gravel crunching under their feet. The cemetery was too quiet, like all sound had been muffled under wet wool. Dylan glanced back once at the grave, marked now only by a temporary placard. The headstone would come later.

"You sure you don't want to come back to our place?" Tommy asked. "Dad's grilling. Mom made that potato salad you like."

"I should head home. Sort through some things."

"Okey dokey." Tommy fished his keys from his

pocket. "But seriously, don't be a hermit. Call me if you need anything. Even if it's just to talk."

About to respond, Dylan stopped when movement caught his eye. A woman stood beside a marble angel statue about fifty yards away, partially hidden by its wing. She wore a dark coat, her hair pulled back. From this distance, in this light…

His heart stopped.

"Mom?" The word slipped out before he could catch it.

Tommy followed his gaze. "What?"

Dylan blinked. The woman shifted a bit, and for one impossible moment, he saw his mother's profile. The same delicate nose, the same way of holding her head when she was thinking. But that was impossible. He'd just buried her.

"Dylan? What is it?"

He looked again. The woman was gone.

"Nothing." He rubbed his eyes with his palm. "Thought I saw… never mind. Just tired."

Tommy studied his face. "You sure you're okay to drive?"

"I'm fine."

But he wasn't. As they reached Tommy's car, Dylan couldn't shake the feeling someone was watching him. The sensation crawled between his shoulder blades like a cold finger tracing his spine.

He turned in a slow circle, scanning the cemetery grounds.

Empty.

"Let's go." Tommy got in his car. "See you at the reception hall."

All Saints' reception hall smelled like coffee and casserole. Dylan sat at a folding table, picking at a paper plate of food while neighbors, coworkers, and church friends shared memories of his mother. He should have been listening, should have been grateful for their kindness. Instead, he kept glancing toward the windows.

One older man approached with a firm handshake and a rough voice that carried unexpected tenderness. "I used to come into the restaurant every day—same booth, same order. Your mom was the only one who ever got it right. I wasn't always... the easiest customer. But she never flinched. Gave it right back when I needed it. In a good way. She had a way of making you feel seen."

"Thank you." Dylan smiled.

The man nodded. "Here's my card with my personal number. Take care now, young man."

After he walked away, Dylan picked up the card

from the table. Frank Rogers, Attorney. He put it in his pocket and resumed eating.

The stories painted a recognizable picture of his mother—kind, hardworking, reliable. But they also highlighted how little these people knew her. No one mentioned her late-night sketching, her rearranging the furniture when she was worried, or her humming while doing dishes.

"Dylan?" Tommy dropped into the chair beside him. "You're not eating."

"Not hungry."

"Mrs. Chen brought those little sandwich things you like." Tommy's eyes narrowed, the same look he'd worn in college when Dylan had struggled through calculus. "How much did you have to borrow?"

"What?"

"For all this." Tommy gestured around the room. "Funeral home, burial plot, catering. Your mom didn't have savings."

Dylan set down his fork. "I didn't borrow anything."

Tommy's eyebrows rose. "Come again?"

"Life insurance. I didn't even know she had a policy." Dylan reached into his jacket pocket and pulled out a folded check stub. "Check came in the mail two days ago."

Tommy took the stub and examined it. "Atlantic Mutual. Never heard of them." He frowned. "Did you file a claim?"

"No. It just showed up."

"That's weird, man. Insurance companies don't usually cut checks before you submit a death certificate and fill out their paperwork. Trust me, I've seen enough estate settlements to know."

Dylan shrugged. "Maybe someone at the hospital called it in. I don't know how these things work. The check cleared. And I looked. It's not one of those scams—once you sign here, you agree to this loan or some such nonsense."

"Still strange." Tommy handed back the stub. "You have all the luck, though. Remember that scholarship? The one you didn't even remember applying for?"

"Oh, come on." Dylan put his hands up. "Do you know how many of those applications I filled out? Mom was so worried the federal grant wouldn't cover everything. You can't expect me to remember every single one."

"No, but..." Tommy cuffed Dylan's shoulder. "Both times, money appeared right when you needed it most."

Before Dylan could respond, Mrs. Patterson approached with a covered dish. "Tuna casserole for later." She set it on the table. "And, honey, I wanted you to know your mother was proud of you. She used to brag about your job, how well you were doing."

"Thank you."

She patted his arm and moved away.

Dylan slid the casserole farther away, throat tight. His mother had been proud of a management trainee position that barely covered his living expenses.

"Ready to go?" Tommy pushed back his chair.

Dylan nodded. As they gathered their things, that watched feeling returned. He glanced toward the church entrance and froze.

A woman stood in the doorway, backlit by afternoon sunlight. Dark hair, familiar posture. She raised one hand, a wave of acknowledgment, then stepped back into the light and disappeared.

"Did you see that?"

Tommy looked toward the door. "See what?"

The doorway stood empty.

Dylan's pulse hammered in his ears. "Nothing. Let's go."

But as they walked to the parking lot, one thought rang clear: *Someone's watching. Someone who looks exactly like Mom.*

CHAPTER 2

COMMUNITY CARE

The insurance check stub lay beside Dylan's laptop, crisp and official-looking. Tommy's words from the funeral echoed in his mind: *That's weird, man.*

Everything seemed weird these days.

The numbers on his laptop screen blurred together, three red cells glaring like warning lights. His phone buzzed on the table. He rubbed the bridge of his nose before answering.

"Yes, I know rent is due on the first. I'm just asking for a little more time. My mom passed away a week ago. I'm still trying to get things in order."

"I'm sorry to hear that. I'll note your account and give you a little space. When you're ready, we can talk about next steps."

"Yeah. Thank you." Dylan disconnected the call and sank into his chair. His fingers tightened around the phone. The kitchen wall across from him would make a satisfying target. He could picture the phone shattering against the faded paint, plastic pieces scattering across the linoleum.

"Breathe through it, Dylan." His mother's voice seemed to whisper from the empty kitchen. *"Surrender to the Lord!"*

He crossed himself and prayed. *Lord, I surrender myself to you. Take care of everything!*

The tension in his shoulders began to ease. When he opened his eyes, the crushing weight in his chest had lifted, replaced by a quiet certainty that he wasn't carrying this burden alone.

He opened his laptop again, the red cells still glaring at him. The bills hadn't disappeared, but somehow, they appeared manageable now.

After graduating from college two years ago, he moved back in with his mom to save money and helped her during her cancer treatments. Now, her absence became a physical hollowness in his chest, a constant reminder she was gone.

He glanced toward the refrigerator, half expecting to see her studying the doctor's appointment magnet, lips moving silently as she confirmed the date and time. *"Pick up your socks!" "Put the dishes in the dishwasher!"* She used to yell at him for leaving things all over the place.

Now, the kitchen sink gave its own scolding. He pushed back his chair to clean up. His mom might not have bothered to decorate the apartment, but she'd kept her place neat and tidy.

As he turned on the faucet, running water triggered something deeper. Her final days in the hospital room flashed unbidden through his mind. The antiseptic smell, the beeping machines, the way her small frame seemed to sink further into the bed with each passing day. He'd held her hand as she slipped away, her fingers cold and fragile in his grasp.

"I'll take care of everything, Mom," he'd promised. *"Don't worry about anything."*

Shaking his head, he chuffed out a breath. How would he keep that promise? The medical bills alone were staggering, and her insurance hadn't covered everything. His credit card debt loomed large, and the rent was already late.

It had always been his mom and him. She'd worked hard as a waitress to support them. Time and time again, he remembered her kneeling by her bed at night to pray. They'd had happy days in the apartment, celebrating his significant events such as confirmation and graduation. She had been thrilled when he snagged one of the few coveted management trainee spots in the two-year program of a well-known regional property management company.

His phone buzzed, interrupting his reminiscing. Not wanting to answer any more calls from the landlord or loan officers, he checked the screen, expecting to swipe the decline icon. But Tommy's contact flashed. They had been best friends since grade school. They'd gone on to the same college but pursued different career paths.

"Yo," Dylan said.

"Hey, are you still moping around?"

"No, I don't mope around."

"Are you dressed? My guess is you're still in your shorts and T-shirt. It's past noon."

He patted his T-shirt. "So? I have time off until tomorrow. Bereavement leave."

"Yeah, I know. But really, how're you holding up?"

"Meh." The one syllable carried everything he couldn't articulate. How could he explain that he woke up every morning forgetting she was gone, only to remember anew each day? That he'd picked up his phone twice already to call her before realizing she wouldn't answer?

"Tell you what. Why don't you get dressed and

come meet me for lunch? I have something for you."

ABOUT THE AUTHOR

S.F. Baumgartner writes fast-paced Christian suspense thrillers. Book 1 of her Mirror Estate series, Living Secrets, was selected as one of the Top Picks in the thriller category at Killer Nashville, 2024. Her love for writing comes second only to her love of reading.

When she's not busy writing about complex characters, secretive operatives, and relentless agents, she spends her time binge-watching crime TV shows, such as NCIS, or playing with her cats. If you enjoy James Patterson's style—specifically short chapters—you'll love her Mirror Estate series.

For all the latest releases and updates, check out her website and subscribe to her newsletter.

ALSO BY S.F. BAUMGARTNER

Mirror Estates series

Buried Secrets, book 1

Living Secrets, book 2

Forgotten Secret, book 3

Tangled Secrets, book 4

Hidden Secrets, book 5

Shadowed Secret, book 6

Box Set (Books 1-4)

Christmas Murders, related novella

Detective KC: Thriller Series

Christmas Murders, a prequel

ACKNOWLEDGMENTS

Publishing a novel is not a solo endeavor, and I'm deeply grateful to those who made this book possible.

A heartfelt thanks to Deirdre Lockhart at Brilliant Cut Editing, Kelsey Darling and Chelsea Lauren from Represent Publishing for their invaluable guidance and support. To the team at 100Covers.com, your stunning cover design perfectly captured the heart of this story.

I also want to thank the amazing beta and ARC readers—your feedback and enthusiasm were crucial in refining this novel.

To my family, your unwavering support has been my greatest strength. And finally, to you, dear readers—this book is for you. Enjoy the journey!

PRAISE FOR BURIED SECRETS - WHERE IT ALL BEGINS: BOOK 1

I felt that the author wove a story that had twists and turns with unexpected moments sprinkled here and there.

— DELPHIA, GOODREADS

They say that dynamite comes in small packages. This one was definitely loaded with plenty of information that will blow your mind.

— TAMMY, GOODREADS

What a great story! This had enough thrill and mystery to draw me in even though it was a short novella.

— MEGAN, GOODREADS

PRAISE FOR LIVING SECRETS: BOOK 2

A great crime novel! Loved that it picked up right where the prequel left off. Loved all the chasing of Lily and who was after her. Loved the cliffhanger and can't wait to read the next one!!

— KRYSTA, GOODREADS

The book is one you will not want to put down, and if you read it at night, you will jump at every noise and check the locks on your doors and windows. Highly recommend.

— BARBARA, GOODREADS

Edge of your seat reading that keeps you guessing until the end. Plenty of drama with twists and turns that keeps you going until the end. Great characters to follow along on this adventure. Good read.

— RHONDA, GOODREADS

PRAISE FOR FORGOTTEN SECRET: BOOK 3

I am exhausted!!! This is an absolute whirlwind and it kept me guessing from the very beginning. I loved Living Secrets and I can safely say, this is even better! I'm not even going to say it's a "one more chapter" book, it's an "I read it in a day book." An amazing plot, great characters, and so many twists and turns your head will spin. I'm loving this series, if you like your fast paced psychological suspense books, give this a go!

— VICKIE, GOODREADS

WOW, TALK ABOUT NEEDING A SCORE CARD TO KEEP TRACK!! I enjoyed Clara's story, and I thought I knew who the culprit was, but I was wrong given all of the players involved! I SURE HOPE

THERE'S ANOTHER BOOK IN THE WORKS!!!

— BECKY, GOODREADS

AWESOME BOOK !!! This is a great psychological suspense thriller that I would recommend to anyone.

— MICHELLE, GOODREADS

PRAISE FOR TANGLED SECRETS: BOOK 4

These books are so addicting—I don't want to do anything else except for finishing the book! The suspense and anticipation was awesome. Getting reacquainted with all of the characters—Olivia, Dylan, Lilly, Ron, Grace, etc. were all great.

— LAURA, GOODREADS

The book has infinite layers, the plot is intriguing and secrets are way too deep. The world is dangerous. The book is filled with twists and turns. The ending shook me.

— RUDRASHREE, GOODREADS

This book had amazing characters, many with secrets that seem to connect them all together. The storyline is intriguing & mysterious. I was always wondering who the person was that had their hands in both sides of the game. The ending left me shocked and ready for the story to continue.

— LUNAWOLFWY, GOODREADS

PRAISE FOR HIDDEN SECRETS: BOOK 5

If there's one thing Baumgartner knows it's suspense. If you haven't already read the first three books of this series, I'd do that. There's a wrap-up/summary of the books at the beginning, which I appreciated, but you'll get a better look at the whole picture and story if you read all of the books in order. Another great story and I can't wait to see what comes next!

— LENA, GOODREADS

What a thrilling ride into this fourth book of the series. The twist and turns keep coming and the secrets keep being revealed. I can't wait to see what is going to happen next as I know there has to be more secrets!! if you enjoy fast paced, being on the edge of your seat reading you will enjoy this series.

— CAROLYN, GOODREADS

I love how fast paced this book is! Once I started it I couldn't put it down. I HAD to know what was going to happen! Between the kidnapping and murders everything was great about this book. There were twists everywhere!

— KRYSTA, GOODREADS

PRAISE FOR SHADOWED SECRET: BOOK 5

The characters, and there were many, are of amazing talent. There is intrigue, deception, betrayal, and lots of danger. The book is a page-turner with many twists and turns. The plot was intriguing and left me trying to guess its many secrets. Unlike other thrillers I've wanted to read, this one had moments of faith and was a clean read. The ending was haunting! Can't wait to read the next one.

— J.E. GRACE, GOODREADS

This is full of action suspense and intrigue so it's right up my alley! I was hooked instantly to this gripping conspiracy thriller! I found the book fast paced and I was on the edge of my seat. I love how all the characters in the book are connected in some way, and it truly has you wondering who is behind everything. It had an open ending so I am excited to see what happens in the next book.

— NIKKI, GOODREADS

The fifth book in one of my favorite series is the best yet. I couldn't put this one down. It has lots of intrigue, mystery, humor, and teamwork. Even though the author gives a brief outline of every book, you should read the previous books first to pick up the nuances. The chart that shows how everyone is interconnected is very helpful, as is the map of the estate. The way the author interweaves storylines is masterful.

— BETTE, GOODREADS

Made in the USA
Middletown, DE
12 September 2025